DEATH AT THE TEACUP INN

ASHFORD CREEK MYSTERY

BOOK ONE

ELLA ANDREW

Copyright © 2025 by Ella Andrew

www.ellaandrew.com

First paperback edition September 2025

Backspace Press

Houston, Texas

Cover design by BACKSPACE PRESS

ISBN 979-8-9932530-3-9 (paperback)

ISBN 979-8-9859898–9-2 (ebook)

Printed in the United States of America

PROLOGUE

SATURDAY MORNING - ONE
WEEK BEFORE THE MURDER

*E*liza Prescott stood in the doorway of Bookmark & Brew, her bookstore and café, breathing in the particular satisfaction that came from perfectly shelved books and fresh-ground coffee. At forty-two, she'd found her rhythm in Ashford Creek—a rhythm that moved between book deliveries, weekend tourists, and the comfortable predictability of small-town life.

"Come on, Bruno," she called to the German Shepherd mix sprawled across the shop's welcome mat. "Time to open."

Bruno, two years into his retirement from the K-9 unit, lifted his graying muzzle with the dignity of a dog who knew his worth. He'd been her partner during her eight years as a detective in Portland, and when early retirement had beckoned—him due to age, her due to a case that had carved too deep—they'd moved to Ashford Creek together.

The bell above her door chimed as Mrs. Henderson entered, punctual as sunrise.

"Eliza, dear! Please tell me the new Louise Penny arrived."

"Yesterday afternoon," Eliza said, producing the book from behind the counter. "I saved you the first copy."

"This is why you're my favorite person in town." Mrs. Henderson clutched the book like treasure. "Don't tell my husband I said that."

As Mrs. Henderson left, Eliza flipped her shop sign to OPEN and surveyed Main Street through the window. Ashford Creek was postcard perfect this morning—flower boxes overflowing with petunias, the old-fashioned lampposts the town council had fought to preserve, and the comforting bustle of Saturday morning routines.

Across the street, the Teacup Inn was already glowing with warm light. Millie Hart waved from the inn's doorway. Eliza waved back, making a mental note to grab lunch there. Millie's lemon scones were legendary, and Saturday was always test batch day for new recipes.

"Eliza! Eliza!" Young Jamie Morrison burst through her door, nearly tripping over Bruno, who side-stepped with practiced ease. "Did you see? Did you see?"

"Breathe, Jamie. What am I supposed to have seen?"

"The newspaper! You're in it!" He thrust the Ashford Creek Gazette at her.

Eliza unfolded it to find her photo on page three under the headline: "Local Bookstore Owner Solves Mystery of Missing Church Funds." The article recounted how she'd noticed discrepancies in the church restoration fundraiser receipts and quietly helped Sheriff Wade trace the theft to the contractor's creative accounting.

"Mom says you're better than the TV detectives," Jamie announced. "'Cause you're real and you have Bruno."

Bruno's tail thumped approval.

"I just noticed something odd," Eliza said, uncomfortable

with the attention. "Sheriff Wade did the real work."

"That's not what he says," a voice said from the doorway.

Wade Colton stood there, tall and solid as an oak, carrying two cups from the inn. "Brought you coffee—that Colombian Geisha blend from the inn. I know you don't carry it here. Millie says it's too expensive for anyone but tourists."

"Bribing me with Millie's special blend?"

"Is it working?" He set the cup on her counter. "I actually came to warn you. Tilda Crane is on the warpath about that article. Says if you can solve the church fund issue, you should investigate who's been spreading 'malicious rumors' about her recipe stealing."

Eliza groaned. Tilda Crane had been the town's self-appointed social arbiter for twenty years, wielding gossip and grudges like weapons. She'd tried to shut down Bookmark & Brew when Eliza first arrived, claiming the town didn't need "outsider businesses."

"She's just upset because the article mentions her nephew was one of the suspects," Eliza said.

"Among other things. She's called a town meeting for next Thursday. Says she has 'revelations that will shake Ashford Creek to its foundations.'"

"How dramatic."

"It's Tilda." Wade sipped his own tea. "Just watch yourself. She doesn't like being upstaged, and solving that theft case put you in the spotlight."

After Wade left, Eliza settled into her morning routine—updating the mystery section, preparing the book club discussion questions, and greeting the steady stream of Saturday customers. It was comfortable, predictable, safe. Everything she'd wanted when she'd left Portland.

Around noon, she closed the shop for lunch and walked to

the Teacup Inn with Bruno. The place was packed, as always on Saturdays. She found her usual table by the window and wasn't surprised when Millie appeared immediately with a plate of scones.

"New recipe," Millie said proudly. "Honey lavender with lemon glaze. Tell me what you think."

Eliza bit into one and closed her eyes. "Perfect. As always."

"Flatterer." Millie beamed. "Oh, Charlie's home from culinary school for the week. He's helping in the Kitchen. Owen's teaching him proper knife skills."

Eliza glanced toward the Kitchen where she could see Owen Kraft, the inn's cook, demonstrating something to Millie's nervous nephew. Owen moved with military precision, every gesture controlled and efficient. He'd appeared in town three years ago, quiet about his past, excellent at his job. Eliza recognized the bearing of someone carrying secrets—it took one to know one.

"Ms. Prescott?" A smooth voice interrupted her thoughts.

A woman stood beside her table—elegant, forties, with the kind of careful composure that suggested practice. "I'm Marina Blackwood. I'm researching Victorian architecture for a book. I heard you're something of a local historian?"

"Hardly. I've only been here two years."

"But you pay attention." Marina's smile didn't reach her eyes. "I can tell. You're a watcher, like me."

Something about the woman set off Eliza's old instincts— the ones from her detective days. But before she could respond, a crash came from across the room.

Tilda Crane had knocked over someone's tea in her dramatic entrance. She stood in the doorway like an actress awaiting applause, her silver hair perfect, her expression thunderous.

"Millie Hart!" she called out. "I demand to know why this establishment is serving MY grandmother's lemon scones without attribution!"

The inn fell silent.

Millie emerged from behind the counter, color high in her cheeks. "Tilda, we've been through this. The recipe was my grandmother's."

"Lies!" Tilda's voice could have etched glass. "And after Thursday's meeting, everyone will know the truth about this inn, about your family, and about everyone else in this town who's been harboring secrets."

She swept her gaze across the room, pausing on Eliza. "Including our newest resident who thinks she's so clever. I know why you really left Portland, Ms. Prescott. Thursday will be very educational for everyone."

She turned and left, leaving arctic silence in her wake.

Eliza felt Bruno press against her leg, a comforting weight. The cozy bubble of her new life suddenly felt very fragile.

"Don't let her rattle you," Millie said quietly. "She threatens everyone."

But as Eliza walked back to her bookstore, she couldn't shake the feeling that something was about to shatter in Ashford Creek. The comfortable rhythm she'd found was about to be broken.

She had no idea how right she was.

One week later, Tilda Crane would be dead, and Eliza would be pulled into a mystery that would reveal just how many secrets lurked beneath the town's picturesque surface.

But for now, it was still Saturday, the sun was shining, and the biggest mystery in Eliza's life was which book to recommend to Mrs. Henderson next.

It was the last truly peaceful day she would have for quite some time.

CHAPTER 1

STORM BREWING

*T*he morning started with Tilda Crane's voice cutting through Main Street like a rusty saw through wet wood.

"Incompetent! Every last one of you."

Eliza Prescott looked up from arranging the new arrivals in her bookstore window, her hands pausing on a pristine copy of the latest Ruth Ware. Through the rain-spotted glass, she could see Tilda standing outside City Hall, waving a manila folder at Mayor Doyle like it was a weapon. Which, knowing Tilda, it probably was.

The bookstore was Eliza's sanctuary, all dark wood shelves and warm lighting, with comfortable reading chairs tucked into corners and the permanent scent of paper and lavender candles. She'd opened Bookmark & Brew two years ago, after leaving Portland, and had carefully cultivated it into exactly the kind of place she'd always wanted to escape into. The mystery section took up the entire north wall, organized not just alphabetically but by subgenre—cozy mysteries at eye level where they sold best, nordic noir brooding on the upper shelves, classic British mysteries in their own special section with burgundy bookends she'd found at an estate sale.

Bruno lifted his head from his bed behind the counter—a custom cushion in police dog blue, a retirement gift from the Portland K-9 unit. His ears swiveled toward the window, tracking the commotion outside, before he gave a questioning whine.

"Just Tilda being Tilda," Eliza told him, returning to her display. She'd gotten in a shipment of the latest Margaret Atwood, and she wanted them prominently featured before the afternoon rush. Though 'rush' was perhaps too strong a word for the gentle flow of customers that kept her business comfortable but never overwhelming.

The morning light through the rain-spotted window cast everything in shades of gray, reminding Eliza of Portland mornings. But Portland had never felt like this—charged with the particular tension that came from too many people knowing too much about each other. She'd been here two years now, long enough to understand that Ashford Creek's postcard prettiness was like fondant on a cake—sweet on the surface, but underneath, the layers held surprises.

The town had been founded in 1842 by textile mill owners who'd wanted to create their own version of paradise. They'd built the Victorian houses that still lined Main Street, established the library that still used its original card catalog system, and created the traditions that governed social life like unwritten laws. The Harvest Festival, the Spring Antique Fair, the Christmas Carol Walk—all orchestrated with the precision of military campaigns and the politics of royal courts.

Tilda Crane had inserted herself into every one of these traditions like a splinter under the skin—painful, persistent, and surprisingly difficult to remove. She'd moved here twenty-five years ago from Boston, newly widowed with old money and new ambitions. Within five years, she'd become the unofficial arbiter of everything from the proper way to arrange flowers for the church altar to who deserved to have their business featured in the tourist brochures.

Eliza had watched it all with an outsider's eye, cataloging the dynamics the way she'd once cataloged evidence. The Henderson sisters, who'd run their antique shop for forty years, always deferred to Tilda in public but rolled their eyes behind her back. Tom Garrett at the pharmacy had a nervous tic that only appeared when Tilda entered his store. Even Mayor Doyle, elected by a landslide three times running, seemed to shrink when Tilda appeared at town meetings with her manila folders and her knowing smile.

She placed the last book and stepped back to admire the arrangement when she noticed something odd. Across the street, people were gathering in small clusters, heads bent together, casting nervous glances toward City Hall. Tom Garrett from the pharmacy stood with Dr. Pemberton, both men looking unusually grave. The Henderson sisters had actually stopped walking their matching Pomeranians to watch Tilda's performance.

Bruno padded over to stand beside her, his solid presence reassuring as always. Two years into retirement, he still moved with the controlled grace of a working dog, seventy pounds of trained muscle and instinct. His muzzle had gone silver, and he was a bit stiff on cold mornings, but his eyes remained sharp, always watching, always evaluating.

"Something's different today, isn't it, boy?" Eliza murmured, scratching behind his ears in the spot that made his back leg twitch.

The bell above her door chimed with its familiar brass song. Millie Hart bustled in, her signature pink scarf fluttering behind her like a distress signal. Millie usually moved with the measured calm of someone who'd run a successful inn for thirty years, but today her steps were quick, agitated.

"Did you hear?" Millie said without preamble, not even pausing to pet Bruno, which was unusual enough to make Eliza truly pay attention. "Tilda's on the warpath again."

"I can see that." Eliza nodded toward the window where Tilda was now jabbing her finger at Patsy Doyle, the mayor's wife. Even from here, Eliza could see Patsy's face flushing red. "What's she upset about now?"

"Everything. Absolutely everything." Millie's hands fluttered like nervous birds. "The antique fair judging, the gazebo renovation, the new parking meters, my lemon scone recipe —" She ticked off on her fingers, each point making her more agitated. "She claims she has 'proof' of some scandal that will 'rain down like judgment' if the mayor doesn't bend to her demands."

Eliza shelved another book, using the familiar motion to study Millie. In two years, she'd never seen the innkeeper this rattled. "She says that every month."

"She came into the inn this morning before dawn—before dawn, Eliza!—demanded to use the private parlor for some kind of meeting today. Said she'd be 'unveiling the truth about this town's dirty secrets today.'"

"Today's Thursday—the town council meeting," Eliza mused, her detective instincts stirring despite her best efforts to keep them dormant.

"Exactly. And she reserved the parlor for right before it." Millie twisted her scarf between her fingers, a gesture Eliza recognized as genuine distress. "Eliza, she looked at me and said, 'Some of us have been keeping secrets about our recipes, haven't we, Millie?' She knows about grandmother's formula."

Eliza's hands stilled on the book she was holding—a vintage Agatha Christie worth more than most people guessed. "Your grandmother's recipe has been in your family for seventy years."

"And it's in my safety deposit box at the bank. The only copy." Millie's voice dropped to a whisper, though they were alone in the shop. "But Tilda had this smile. You know the one —like a cat that's already eaten the canary and is just waiting for you to notice the feathers."

"She's bluffing," Eliza said firmly, though something cold was settling in her stomach. "That recipe is what makes the inn special. She couldn't have—"

"But what if she photographed it somehow? Or bribed someone at the bank? You know how she is." Millie's voice cracked slightly. "And I'm not the only one she's threatening. Charlie's terrified she'll expose his scholarship issues. Owen thinks she knows about his record. Even that new woman who's been hanging around—Marina something—Tilda pulled her aside yesterday and whispered something that made her go white as bone."

The door chimed again with more force than necessary. Charlie Harris, Millie's nineteen-year-old nephew, stumbled in looking like he'd seen a ghost. His culinary school uniform was rumpled, flour dusting his sleeve and caught in his black hair. There was a smudge of what looked like chocolate on his jaw, and his eyes had the wild look of someone running on no sleep and too much coffee.

"Aunt Millie, she's coming to the inn. Right now. She says she wants the 'special treatment' for her tea." His voice cracked on the last word, breaking like he was thirteen instead of nineteen. "She had that look."

"What look?" Eliza asked, though she suspected she knew.

"Like a cat that's cornered a whole family of mice," Charlie said miserably. "She knows about the admission essay. I know she does. She kept making comments about 'creative writing' and 'fiction versus truth' when she saw me at the grocery store yesterday."

Millie squared her shoulders, visibly pulling herself together. "Well, we'll give her our finest service, as always. Kill her with kindness, that's what grandmother always said."

Eliza winced at the unfortunate turn of phrase. "I'll come with you. I need a break from inventory anyway, and Bruno's been eyeing the door for the past hour."

Bruno's tail thumped agreement, already moving toward the door with the eagerness of a dog who knew the inn meant potential treats.

Eliza grabbed her raincoat from the hook by the door—a practical navy that had served her well in Portland and was proving equally useful in Ashford Creek's temperamental spring weather. She flipped the shop sign to "Back at Three" and locked the door, though crime in Ashford Creek usually extended no further than teenagers sneaking beer and the occasional tourist shoplifting postcards.

They crossed Main Street together as the morning mist began to thicken into proper rain. The cobblestones—the town council's pride and the road department's nightmare—gleamed like oil in the wet. The Teacup Inn glowed warmly at the corner, its Victorian gingerbread trim and leaded glass windows making it look like something from a fairy tale.

The inn had been built in 1892 by a railroad magnate's widow who'd wanted to create "a place of refinement and grace in the wilderness." What had been wilderness then was now downtown Ashford Creek, but the inn maintained its air of genteel hospitality. The painted exterior was a symphony of cream, sage green, and dusty rose, colors Millie had agonized over for months before the last restoration. Even in the gray morning, it looked inviting.

The chalkboard under the awning—Millie's one concession to modern marketing—read in Charlie's artistic script: Rainy Day Special - Lemon scones with our signature glaze, clotted cream, and exceptional service.

"I should change that," Millie muttered. "Take out the 'signature' part before she sees it."

"Don't you dare," Eliza said. "That's letting her win."

Inside, the inn was already half-full despite the early hour. The antique fair had brought tourists, their voices creating a pleasant hum against the clink of china and silver. But the locals had gathered in worried clusters, and Eliza could feel the undercurrent of tension like electricity before a storm.

The interior was everything the exterior promised—warm wood paneling, William Morris wallpaper in the front parlor, Turkish rugs worn soft by generations of feet. The tea room opened to the right, round tables dressed in crisp white linens with small vases of fresh flowers at each center. Today's flowers were yellow roses from Millie's own garden, their cheerful color at odds with the mood.

Eliza recognized the usual suspects: the Hendersons whispering over their Earl Grey at their customary table by the bay window, Dr. Pemberton hiding behind his newspaper in the corner like a turtle in his shell, and in the far corner, the mysterious Marina—a sleek woman in her forties who'd appeared in town two weeks ago claiming to be researching Victorian architecture but who seemed more interested in the townspeople than the buildings.

Marina sat alone, as always, drinking tea with precise, measured sips. She wore black today—elegant slacks and a cashmere sweater that looked expensive. Her dark hair was pulled into a neat chignon, and she had the kind of posture that suggested ballet lessons or military training. Maybe both.

Owen Kraft moved between the kitchen and dining room with practiced efficiency, his military bearing evident in every economical movement. He navigated the tight spaces between tables without ever brushing against a chair or customer, each plate balanced perfectly, each cup set down without a sound. The burn scar on his left hand caught the light as he set down a tray at the Henderson's table. He'd been Millie's cook for three years now, ever since his dishonorable discharge— though Millie was the only one who'd hired him despite the whispers about what had happened at Fort Bragg.

"Ladies," he said to the Hendersons with a slight nod, his voice carrying just enough warmth to be polite but not enough to invite conversation.

"She's here," Charlie whispered urgently, and sure enough, Tilda Crane swept through the door like she owned the place.

At sixty-three, Tilda had the kind of sharp, preserved beauty that came from expensive face creams and sheer spite. Her silver hair was pulled into a perfect chignon that had probably taken an hour to achieve but was meant to look effortless. Her tweed suit—Chanel, if Eliza's eye was correct— was impeccable despite the rain. She carried herself like visiting royalty forced to mingle with peasants, her posture so rigid it could have been used as a architectural level.

She paused in the doorway, letting everyone notice her

arrival, her pale blue eyes scanning the room like a predator cataloging prey.

"Millie," she announced, loud enough for everyone to hear. "I'll take my usual table. And do bring out your best china—the Spode, not that department store nonsense you use for tourists. I'm expecting someone special at eleven." She glanced at her Cartier watch with theatrical precision. "That gives you ninety minutes to impress me. I'm sure you'll want to, given what's at stake."

Patsy Doyle, who'd followed Tilda in, her face still flushed from their confrontation outside, bristled visibly. "Tilda, you can't keep threatening—"

"Can't I?" Tilda's smile was arctic, her voice carrying the kind of cultured menace that had been perfected in finishing schools. "Your husband seems to think that gazebo can stay half-painted through the antique fair. I have photographs that suggest his renovation budget went somewhere far more... personal. That weekend in Burlington, perhaps? The charges at the jewelry store? Shall I continue?"

Patsy's face flushed red, then drained white. Her mouth opened and closed like a landed fish.

"Your table is ready, Mrs. Crane," Millie said smoothly, though Eliza could see her hands trembling slightly. "Charlie will show you up to the private parlor."

"The private parlor?" Dr. Pemberton looked up from his paper, his reading glasses sliding down his nose. "Bit grand for morning tea, isn't it?"

Tilda's eyes glittered with malicious pleasure. "I prefer privacy for certain conversations. One never knows who might be listening." Her gaze swept the room, pausing meaningfully on each face. "Isn't that right, Marina?"

The elegant stranger in the corner stiffened slightly, her

15

teacup pausing halfway to her lips, but she continued sipping without responding. Only someone watching closely—as Eliza was—would have noticed the slight tremor in her hand.

"Charlie," Tilda commanded, her voice cracking like a whip. "My tea. Earl Grey, properly steeped—four minutes, not a second more or less. And I'll have one of your aunt's special lemon scones. The ones with the signature glaze that everyone raves about." Her emphasis on 'signature' made Millie flinch. "I'm quite particular about my glazes, you know. I've been experimenting with my own. In fact, I brought a sample for comparison."

She produced a small glass jar from her handbag with the flourish of a magician revealing a rabbit. The jar was crystal, old-fashioned, with a silver lid that caught the light. Inside, white crystals glinted like crushed diamonds. "My special sugar blend. Adds just a hint of almond essence to complement the lemon. I insist you try it on my scone. Call it... a peace offering."

Charlie took the jar with shaking hands, holding it like it might explode. "Yes, Mrs. Crane."

"And Charlie?" Tilda's voice turned silky, dangerous. "Do make sure you use it. I'll know if you don't. I always know."

As Tilda climbed the stairs to the private parlor, her heels clicking against the wood in a rhythm that sounded like a countdown, conversation exploded in her wake.

"That woman is pure poison," someone muttered from a corner table.

"Someone should do something about her," another voice added, low and bitter.

"Did you hear what she said about the Mayor? And that jewelry store business?"

"Burlington? But that's where his mother lives..."

16

"Ladies," Millie called out, her innkeeper's voice cutting through the gossip. "We sip. We do not spar. Not with porcelain in hand."

Eliza slid into the window seat, her favorite spot where she could observe both the tea room and the street outside. Bruno flopped under the table with a deep sigh, his body creating a warm weight against her feet, paws crossed like a gentleman. The rain had picked up, drumming against the glass in an irregular rhythm that made her think of codes and secrets.

She watched the room's dynamics with her detective's eye, a habit she couldn't quite shake even after two years of civilian life. Owen had returned to the Kitchen but kept glancing toward the stairs. Marina had pulled out a small notebook and was writing something in quick, sharp strokes. The Hendersons huddled closer together, their Pomeranians picking up on the tension and whining softly.

Millie arrived with a tray, her movements less graceful than usual. "Your usual—English Breakfast with milk, no sugar," she said, setting down the cup with a slight rattle. "And lemon scones. On the house. I need friendly faces today."

"What's this about Marina?" Eliza asked quietly, glancing at the woman in question.

"She showed up two weeks ago, said she was writing a book about Victorian architecture. But yesterday, Tilda cornered her in the post office. I couldn't hear what was said, but Marina left looking shaken." Millie lowered her voice further, leaning in close enough that Eliza could smell her lavender hand cream. "And here's the strange thing—I could swear I've seen Marina before, years ago. Maybe at one of the summer festivals? But she insists this is her first time in Ashford Creek."

Before Eliza could respond, a crash came from the Kitchen, followed by raised voices. The sound of metal hitting the floor, then angry words.

"I won't do it!" Charlie's voice, high and strained, carrying clearly through the service door.

"You will, or you'll find another job." Owen's deeper rumble, authoritative but with an edge of something else—fear?

Millie hurried toward the Kitchen, her scarf fluttering behind her. Eliza followed, Bruno padding silently beside her, his ears pricked forward in alert mode.

They found Charlie holding a tray with Tilda's tea service, his face pale as parchment. The Spode china—white with delicate blue flowers—rattled slightly from the tremor in his hands. Owen stood blocking his path to the stairs, solid as a wall, arms crossed over his broad chest.

"She wants her special sugar on the scone," Charlie said, his voice barely above a whisper. "But something seems off about it. It smells wrong."

Owen took the jar, unscrewed the lid with quick, efficient movements, and sniffed. His expression darkened, the scar on his hand standing out white against his skin. "Bitter almonds," he said quietly, immediately sealing the jar and setting it down carefully. "That's not sugar blend.

"What do you mean?" Millie asked, though her face suggested she already suspected.

Owen's jaw tightened, a muscle jumping in his cheek. "In the service, we were trained to recognize certain... substances. Chemical weapons, poisons. This smells like—" He stopped himself, glancing at Charlie. "We shouldn't use this."

"But she'll raise hell if we don't," Charlie protested, his voice climbing. "You know she will. She'll tell everyone about

—" He caught himself, glancing at Eliza with the guilty look of someone who'd almost revealed a secret.

"About what?" Eliza asked gently, using her interview voice—the one that had gotten countless witnesses to open up.

CHAPTER 2

*C*harlie's shoulders slumped in defeat. "I... I had help with my culinary school admission essay. Not cheating exactly, but... a service that 'polished' it. Made it sound better than anything I could write. Tilda found out somehow. She's been holding it over me for weeks, threatening to tell the school board."

"And you?" Eliza looked at Owen, who'd gone still as stone.

Owen's expression was granite. "My business is my own." But his hand had moved unconsciously to his side, where Eliza recognized the tell-tale adjustment of someone used to carrying a weapon.

We'll use regular sugar," Millie decided, her voice firm with the authority of three decades of hospitality. "She won't know the difference." "She will," Charlie said miserably. "She always knows. She's like a bloodhound for deception."

A bell tinkled from upstairs—the private parlor's service bell, an antique pull-cord system Millie had preserved. It rang again, more insistent, imperious demand in every chime.

"I'll take it up," Owen said, reaching for the tray.

"No," Charlie straightened, squaring his thin shoulders. "It's my job. I'll face her." He took the tray and headed for the stairs. At the last second, despite Millie's decision, he grabbed Tilda's jar too knowing she'd check, knowing she'd make his life hell if he didn't follow her exact instructions. His footsteps on the old wood sounded like a funeral march, slow and measured. Each step creaked slightly—the third, the seventh, and the tenth, Eliza noted automatically.

Bruno tensed beside her, a low whine escaping his throat. His ears swiveled toward the stairs, tracking something, and his body shifted into what Eliza recognized as his alert stance.

"What is it, boy?" she asked, her hand finding his collar.

Before Bruno could offer more warning, they heard Charlie's voice from above, tight with fear: "Mrs. Crane? Your tea is—oh my God. Oh my God!"

The crash of the tray was thunderous in the morning quiet. China shattered, silver rang against wood, and Charlie's scream echoed through the inn like a siren.

Eliza ran for the stairs, muscle memory from eight years of police work taking over. Bruno stayed at her heel, trained to follow but not interfere. She took the stairs two at a time, noting absently that Charlie had been right—the third, seventh, and tenth steps did creak. The hallway at the top was dim, lit only by a small window at the end that looked out onto the rain-swept street.

The private parlor door stood wide open like a mouth frozen in surprise.

The scene inside was almost peaceful, except for Charlie pressed against the doorframe, hyperventilating, his hands clutching the wood so hard his knuckles were white. The tea service lay scattered across the Persian rug—a nineteenth-century Tabriz that Millie had inherited from her grandmother. Tea was spreading in a dark stain, and broken china glinted like teeth in the morning light.

Tilda Crane sat in the wingback chair by the window, her posture perfect, her eyes open and staring at nothing. The rain on the window behind her created moving shadows across her face, giving the illusion of expression where there was none. Her fingers still curled around a delicate china cup, frozen in an eternal toast. On the plate beside her, a single lemon scone sat with one bite missing, its signature glaze pooling like liquid sunshine.

The room smelled of lemon, Earl Grey, and underneath it all—cutting through the comfortable scents like a blade—the distinct smell of bitter almonds.

Eliza's detective instincts kicked in, cataloging details with the automatic precision of eight years in Portland homicide. The teacup in Tilda's hand was from the Spode collection— she could see the blue flowers clearly, no chips or cracks, positioned as if Tilda had been about to take another sip. The angle suggested Tilda had been relaxed, unsuspecting. No defensive wounds on her visible skin, no signs of struggle. The chair hadn't moved—the indentations in the Persian rug showed it had been in the same position for hours.

The morning light from the window created a tableau that would have been peaceful if not for the absolute stillness of death. Tilda's tweed suit showed no wrinkles beyond normal wear, her pearl necklace sat perfectly centered. Even her hair, that silver chignon she spent an hour perfecting each morning according to town gossip, remained intact. Only her face betrayed the violence of her end—the slight blue tinge to her lips, the pupils fixed and dilated, the expression of surprise that suggested whatever she'd expected from this morning, death hadn't been it.

The sugar crystals scattered on the rug formed an almost perfect arc, as if someone had thrown them in haste or anger. Eliza counted approximately two tablespoons' worth, enough to thoroughly sweeten a cup of tea or, in this case, deliver a fatal dose of poison. The jar itself, crystal with its ornate silver lid, had rolled to rest against the settee's carved leg, leaving a thin trail of white crystals like a comet's tail across the dark wool.

Bruno growled low in his throat, hackles raised as he stared at the body. His training kept him back, but every line of his body radiated tension.

Tilda Crane's reign of terror over Ashford Creek had come to an abrupt end.

And as Eliza looked at the scattered sugar crystals glinting on the carpet like a constellation of guilt, the overturned jar that had rolled under the settee, and the expression of surprise frozen on Tilda's face, she realized that someone in this inn had just committed murder.

The question was: who had Tilda pushed too far?

Thunder cracked overhead, rattling the old windows in their frames, and the lights flickered once, casting shadows that seemed to dance around Tilda's still form. For a moment, in the shifting light, Tilda's expression seemed to change— surprise to accusation, as if even in death she was cataloging one last secret.

"Nobody move," Eliza commanded, her voice carrying the authority of her former career. The cop she'd tried to leave behind in Portland was suddenly, fully present. "Charlie, call 911. Everyone else, stay exactly where you are."

But as she turned to secure the scene, something made her freeze. She noticed something that made her blood run cold, a detail that would trouble her through the investigation to come.

The parlor's service door—the one that led to the back stairs, the one that should have been locked—stood slightly ajar. The darkness beyond it seemed to breathe.

Someone had been here. Someone had watched Tilda die.

And that someone was still in the inn.

CHAPTER 3

SECRETS IN THE STEAM

he Ashford Creek Police Department consisted of exactly four people, and Sheriff Wade Colton was worth at least three of them on his own. He arrived within seven minutes of Charlie's call, rain streaming off his brown sheriff's hat like a waterfall, his presence immediately transforming chaos into something manageable.

Eliza heard him before she saw him—the authoritative tread of his boots on the inn's front steps, the low rumble of his voice directing his deputies, the way the crowd noise below shifted from panic to nervous compliance. Wade had that effect on people. At six-foot-two with shoulders that suggested his college football days weren't entirely behind him, he commanded attention without trying. But it was his eyes—steady gray, patient but sharp—that really did the work.

"Nobody leaves," he announced, his deep voice carrying through the establishment like rolling thunder. "Deputy Lang, secure the exits. Deputy Morris, start a sign-in sheet. Everyone who was here when it happened stays here."

Deputy Lang, young and eager with academy polish still

on him, immediately moved to the front door. Deputy Morris, older and more weathered, pulled out a notebook and began corralling the tourists who were edging toward escape.

Eliza stood guard at the parlor door, Bruno sitting at attention beside her. She'd already prevented three people from contaminating the scene—Patsy Doyle ("I just need to see if she's really..."), Dr. Pemberton ("I'm a doctor, I should check for signs of life"), and Marina, who'd appeared silently on the stairs without explanation, her approach so quiet even Bruno had only noticed her at the last second.

"Eliza," Wade said, climbing toward her. His eyes held a mixture of respect and resignation, the look of a man who'd just had his morning complicated in a familiar way. "Should have known you'd be here."

"Pure coincidence," she said.

"With you, it never is." He studied the scene from the doorway, his weathered face growing more grave with each detail. She watched him catalog everything—the position of the body, the scattered tea service, the morning light playing across Tilda's frozen expression. His hand moved unconsciously to his belt where his radio sat, then away, a tell that he was thinking hard.

"Tell me what you saw," he said.

Eliza gave him the rundown: Tilda's threats, the mysterious jar of "special sugar," Charlie's discovery of the body, the service door ajar. She used her cop voice, the one she'd thought she'd retired—just facts, no interpretation, each detail in chronological order. Wade listened without interrupting, occasionally nodding, his eyes never leaving the scene.

"This jar," he said when she finished. "Where is it now?"

Eliza pointed to where it had rolled under the settee, just

visible in the shadow. "Nobody's touched it since Charlie dropped the tray."

Wade pulled on latex gloves from his belt pouch—he always carried them, a habit from thirty years of law enforcement. He moved into the room with careful steps, avoiding the broken china, and crouched by the settee. His knees popped audibly, and he grimaced.

"Getting too old for this," he muttered, carefully retrieving the jar. A few crystals still clung to the rim, catching the light like tiny diamonds. He sniffed carefully, his training showing in the way he wafted the scent rather than breathing directly, then pulled back sharply. "Cyanide, most likely. The bitter almond smell is distinctive. Seen it twice before—once in Portland during that insurance fraud case, once here about fifteen years back."

"She brought it herself," Eliza said. "Called it her special sugar blend. Insisted Charlie use it on her scone."

Wade's eyebrows rose, creating deep lines in his forehead. "She brought her own murder weapon?"

"That's what it looks like. But Wade..." Eliza lowered her voice, glancing back at the dim hallway. "That service door was open. Someone else was here."

Wade moved to the service door, examining it without touching. The old brass hinges were well-oiled—Millie's attention to detail—and wouldn't have squeaked. Someone could have stood there, watching, without anyone knowing.

Before Wade could respond, a commotion erupted downstairs. Deputy Morris's voice rose above the noise, surprisingly commanding for such a soft-spoken man: "Ma'am, you can't go up there!"

Marina appeared on the landing, having somehow slipped past the deputy. She moved like water, silent and fluid, but her usual composure had cracked. Her elegant hands trembled as she clutched her leather bag—expensive, Italian, the kind that cost more than most people's rent. Her dark eyes darted between Wade and Eliza.

"Sheriff, I need to speak with you privately," she said. Her accent, which Eliza hadn't noticed before, showed slightly— just a hint of something West Coast, maybe Seattle. "It's about Tilda. About why she—" She stopped, noticing Eliza, and her expression shuttered. "Alone, please."

Wade studied her for a long moment, his cop eyes taking in details—the slight smudge in her lipstick, the way her right hand kept moving to her bag, the tension in her shoulders. "In a minute, Ms...?"

"Blackwood. Marina Blackwood." The name came out practiced, automatic.

"Ms. Blackwood. Please return downstairs. I'll speak with everyone shortly."

Marina hesitated, her gaze flicking to the parlor door where Tilda's foot was just visible. Something passed across her face—not grief exactly, but something more complex. Relief mixed with fear, perhaps. Then she descended, her heels silent on the stairs that had creaked under Charlie's feet.

Wade turned back to the parlor, pulling out his phone. "I need to call the state police. This is beyond our usual—"

"You can handle this," Eliza said quietly. "You've done it before."

"Not with half the town as suspects," Wade replied, but he pocketed his phone. Instead, he pulled out a digital camera and began his methodical documentation. Each angle, each piece of evidence, each detail captured with the patience of someone who knew that murders were solved in the details, not the drama.

"Eliza, I need you downstairs too," he said without looking up from his work. "This is an active crime scene."

"Of course." She started to go, then paused. "Wade, there's something else. Charlie mentioned Tilda was expecting someone at eleven. It's only ten-thirty."

Wade checked his watch, a sturdy Timex that had survived three decades of police work, frowning. "So either she decided to sample her own poisoned scone before her guest arrived, or—"

"Or someone else knew about the poison and made sure she ate it first," Eliza finished.

Their eyes met, and she saw him mentally shift from small-town sheriff dealing with a sudden death to investigator working a murder case. It was like watching a blade being drawn from a sheath—sudden, sharp, and somehow inevitable.

Downstairs, the tea room had transformed into a makeshift interrogation center. Deputy Lang had closed the curtains, giving the room an underwater quality in the gray morning light. Deputy Morris had commandeered the largest table and was methodically taking names and contact information, his printing neat and precise. The tourists—a family of four from Connecticut and an elderly couple from Boston —huddled by the door looking bewildered and slightly offended, as if murder was not what they'd paid for in their Ashford Creek vacation packages.

The locals had instinctively separated into their usual groups, but with a new wariness. They watched each other now with different eyes—not neighbors, but suspects.

Millie stood behind the counter, mechanically polishing the same teacup over and over, the motion hypnotic. The cup was one of her grandmother's—bone china so thin you could see light through it. "I can't believe she's dead," she kept saying to no one in particular. "In my inn. In grandmother's parlor. The Queen stayed in that room in 1959. Did you know that? The Queen, and now..."

Charlie sat in the corner, still pale and shaking, his culinary school uniform now splattered with tea stains that looked disturbingly like blood in the dim light. Owen stood beside him, arms crossed, expression unreadable. But Eliza noticed how he'd positioned himself—between Charlie and everyone else, protective. Every few seconds, Owen's eyes would flick to the stairs, then to the exits, like he was calculating distances, planning escapes or defenses.

"Where did the jar come from?" Deputy Morris was asking Charlie, his voice gentle but insistent. "Did Mrs. Crane give it directly to you?"

"Y-yes," Charlie stammered. His hands twisted in his lap, leaving flour residue on his dark pants. "She pulled it from her purse. Said to use it on her scone specifically. Said it would enhance the flavor profile." He laughed, a broken sound. "Flavor profile. She murdered herself over a flavor profile."

"You did exactly what she requested," Owen said firmly, his hand landing on Charlie's shoulder. "If anyone's responsible, it's—" He cut himself off, jaw clenching.

"It's who?" Morris pressed, pen poised.

Owen's jaw tightened further, the muscles visible beneath his weathered skin. "Nothing. I misspoke."

Eliza settled at her previous table, Bruno alert beneath it. His ears swiveled constantly, tracking every movement, every voice. She watched the room's dynamics with her investigator's instincts, cataloguing every nervous tic and furtive glance.

Patsy Doyle kept checking her phone, her thumb moving in repetitive swipes even though the screen was dark. Dr. Pemberton had developed a suspicious interest in the window, despite the rain obscuring any view. He'd adjusted his glasses seventeen times in the past minute—Eliza had counted. Marina sat alone, her tea untouched and now certainly cold, staring at something in her bag with an expression of profound loss.

Wade's interview technique hadn't changed much since Eliza had known him in Portland, where their paths had crossed on several cases. He had a way of creating silence that made people want to fill it, a patient stillness that suggested he had all the time in the world to wait for the truth. She watched him now as he observed the room, his gray eyes taking in every nervous gesture, every exchanged glance, every tell that might lead to answers.

The inn itself seemed to be holding its breath. The usual sounds—the comfortable clink of china, the whisper of turning newspaper pages, the gentle bubble of conversation—had been replaced by a watchful quiet. Even the building seemed to sense the weight of what had happened. The old radiators, usually prone to cheerful clanking, had gone silent. The grandfather clock in the corner, a donation from the founding family that had kept perfect time for over a century, seemed to tick more slowly, each second drawn out like taffy.

Eliza noticed how people had unconsciously arranged themselves into camps. The locals clustered together near the windows, as if proximity to escape routes might offer comfort. The staff—what remained of them—huddled near the kitchen door, their usual efficient movements replaced by uncertain stillness.

Dr. Pemberton hadn't moved from his corner table in

forty-five minutes, but his coffee cup had been refilled three times—Eliza had counted. His hands, surgeon's hands that she'd seen steady as stone during medical emergencies, trembled slightly each time he lifted the cup. The newspaper in front of him hadn't been turned in all that time, though he maintained the pretense of reading, his eyes scanning the same headline over and over.

The Henderson sisters whispered to each other in the rapid-fire shorthand of siblings who'd spent seventy years together. Their Pomeranians, usually perfectly behaved, whined and pulled at their leashes, sensing the distress their owners tried to hide. Mrs. Henderson's hands kept moving to her purse, checking for something—her phone, perhaps, or just the nervous gesture of someone who needed to be doing something, anything, other than sitting still while murder hung in the air like morning fog.

Tilda had been systematically destroying lives, and everyone in the room knew it. The Henderson sisters' antique shop had been under siege for months over a Victorian armoire that Tilda claimed was a fake—a claim that, if proven, would ruin their reputation with collectors from Boston to Burlington. Tom Garrett faced even worse—Tilda's accusations about overcharging seniors and her threats to report him to the state board could end his thirty-year career with a single phone call. And Rebecca Harris, who'd arrived just minutes before the discovery, kept her distance from her son Charlie, as if proximity might reveal whatever secret had brought her here this morning—her timing either terrible or suspicious.

Rebecca was a small woman, neat and contained, but her hands betrayed her—they kept moving to her grandmother's ruby ring, twisting it, a gesture Eliza recognized as severe anxiety.

"Ladies and gentlemen," Wade announced, having come back downstairs. His presence immediately commanded attention, conversations dying mid-sentence. "I need to interview each of you individually. We'll use the library. Deputy Lang will call you one at a time."

"This is ridiculous," Patsy burst out, her voice climbing to a pitch that made Bruno's ears flatten. "Tilda poisoned herself! She brought the jar, she insisted on using it. Case closed. We all saw it. Charlie's not to blame—she is!"

"Then why was the service door open?" Eliza asked mildly.

Everyone turned to stare at her. The question hung in the air like an accusation.

Patsy flushed. "What door?"

"The parlor has two entrances," Eliza explained, using her teaching voice, the one that had served her well in countless witness interviews. "The main door from the front stairs, and a service door that connects to the back stairs—the ones staff use. That door was open when we found her, but Charlie came up the front stairs."

"So?" Tom Garrett asked, but his voice had an edge of worry.

"So someone else was in that room. Either while Tilda was dying, or just after."

A ripple of unease went through the crowd like wind through wheat. People shifted, looking at each other with new suspicion. The Henderson sisters actually scooted their chairs slightly apart, as if suddenly unsure of each other.

"That's enough speculation," Wade said firmly, though Eliza caught the slight nod he gave her—approval and warning mixed. "Mr. Harris, you're first."

As Charlie was led away, walking like a man heading to execution, Millie approached Eliza's table. She'd stopped polishing the cup, but her hands still trembled slightly.

"The service door," she whispered, leaning close enough that Eliza could smell her rose hand lotion mixed with nervous sweat. "I locked it this morning. I always lock it when we're using the parlor for special guests. It's part of my routine—check the flowers, adjust the curtains, lock the service door."

"Who has keys?"

"Just me, Owen, and Charlie. We keep a spare in the Kitchen, but..." She frowned, creating lines around her mouth that hadn't been there this morning. "Actually, I haven't seen it in a few days. I noticed on Monday when I went to get it for the cleaning service."

Before Eliza could respond, Bruno suddenly stood, ears pricked forward, body tense. He was staring at Marina's table with the fixed attention that meant he'd noticed something important. The woman had pulled something from her bag— a photograph, old and creased along the edges. She studied it intently, her lips moving as if in prayer or curse.

Eliza rose and crossed to her, Bruno padding alongside. Marina didn't look up until Eliza's shadow fell across the photograph.

"Ms. Blackwood?"

Marina startled, quickly shoving the photo back in her bag. But not before Eliza caught a glimpse: a group of young women in front of what looked like the Teacup Inn, circa twenty years ago, the colors faded but the faces clear. One of them could have been a younger Marina—same bone structure, same elegant posture. Another looked remarkably like Tilda, though decades younger and actually smiling.

"You knew her," Eliza said quietly, sitting down uninvited. "From before."

Marina's composure finally cracked completely. Her face crumpled like tissue paper, years of practiced control dissolving. "You don't understand. Tilda destroyed my life twenty years ago. My business, my marriage, everything. All because I had something she wanted."

"What did she want?" Eliza asked.

Marina laughed bitterly, the sound sharp as broken glass. "A recipe. Can you believe it? A stupid recipe for lemon scones that won a national competition. She accused me of stealing it from her, launched a campaign that ruined my bakery's reputation. Health department inspections every week, rumors about expired ingredients, anonymous reviews online before online even mattered." Her hands clenched. "I had to leave town, change my name, start over. I lost everything because of a few cups of flour and sugar."

"And you came back now because...?"

"Because I heard she was finally going to get what she deserved. Someone sent me a letter saying Tilda's crimes would be exposed at the town meeting. That justice would be served." Marina's eyes glittered with unshed tears. "I wanted to see it happen. I wanted to watch her fall."

"Who sent the letter?"

"I don't know. It was unsigned. Block printing, generic paper."

Eliza felt the pieces clicking together, but the picture was still incomplete. "Marina, I need to see that letter."

"I burned it," Marina said quickly. Too quickly. Her tell was subtle—the slight touch to her bag, unconscious protection of something still there.

Before Eliza could press further, a scream echoed from the

Kitchen. Not terror this time—surprise and disgust mixed. Everyone jumped up, chairs scraping against wood, rushing toward the sound.

They found Rebecca Harris standing by the pantry, pointing at the floor with a shaking hand. A steady drip of red was pooling beneath the door, viscous and spreading.

Owen pushed past everyone with military efficiency and yanked the door open. A body tumbled out—

But it wasn't a person. It was one of Millie's cloth napkins, soaked in what looked like blood but smelled like—

"Raspberry jam," Owen announced, holding up the dripping fabric with two fingers, his expression disgusted. "Someone's idea of a joke."

But Rebecca wasn't looking at the napkin anymore. She was staring into the pantry itself, where someone had written on the back wall in the same red jam, the letters dripping like something from a horror movie: SHE KNEW TOO MUCH. THE TRUTH DIES WITH HER.

CHAPTER 4

THE SERVICE DOOR

"*T*hursday is today," Patsy breathed, her face pale. "That's when Tilda was going to reveal her 'proof.'"

Wade pushed through the crowd, his expression thunderous. "Everyone out of the Kitchen. Now."

As people filed out, Eliza noticed Charlie wasn't among them. "Where's Charlie?" she asked Millie.

"Still being interviewed, I think—" Millie stopped, frowning. "No, wait. Wade just sent him to fetch his notebook from the library."

They found Charlie in the library, standing frozen over Wade's interview notes. The library was a small room, really just a converted parlor, but Millie had filled it with books donated by guests over the years. Charlie stood by the writing desk, his face had gone from pale to green, like old cheese.

"Charlie?" Millie rushed to him. "What's wrong?"

He held up a piece of paper with trembling hands. It wasn't from Wade's notebook. It was a note, written in Tilda's distinctive handwriting—sharp, angular, unmistakable:

Marina Blackwood is really Mary Brennan. She killed her husband in Seattle five years ago. Suspected poisoning but never proven. She's here for revenge because she thinks I'm responsible for his death. But she's wrong. The real killer is someone she'd never suspect. Someone who's been here all along. If something happens to me, check the sugar jar—but not the one I brought. Check the one that was already here.

Eliza's blood ran cold. "There were two jars?"

Charlie nodded miserably. "Tilda brought one, but there was already one in the parlor. The tea service we set up this morning—it had a matching sugar jar. I thought it was empty, but..."

"But you used Tilda's jar, right?" Eliza pressed.

"I... I think so? They looked the same. Crystal with silver lids. I grabbed one from the tray, but in the nervousness of it all..." His voice trailed off, hands wringing.

Wade appeared in the doorway, having heard the commotion. He read the note, his expression darkening like storm clouds gathering. "Where's Ms. Blackwood?"

They rushed back to find Marina's table empty, her teacup cold and abandoned, her coat gone. The front door stood slightly open, rain blowing in, creating puddles on Millie's polished floor.

"She ran," Deputy Morris reported, slightly out of breath. "Must have slipped out during the pantry commotion. I tried to follow but she had a head start."

"Find her," Wade ordered. Then, to the room at large: "Nobody else moves."

But Eliza was already moving, Bruno at her side. Because she'd noticed something others hadn't—wet footprints leading not out the front door, but up the back stairs. The prints were small, elegant—Marina's expensive Italian boots. She hadn't fled.

She'd gone back to the scene of the crime.

Eliza climbed the service stairs quietly, Bruno padding silently behind her. His training kicked in—he knew when to be invisible. The old wood was damp from various feet, muffling their approach. The door to the parlor stood open, afternoon light struggling through rain-streaked windows.

Inside, Marina knelt by Tilda's chair, searching frantically through the dead woman's pockets. Her elegant composure was completely gone—she looked desperate, wild, her perfect hair coming loose from its chignon.

"Looking for this?" Eliza asked.

Marina spun around. In Eliza's hand was a small key, one she'd noticed earlier attached to Tilda's bracelet—a detail her detective's eye had catalogued automatically.

"That's not—" Marina started.

"Your husband's safety deposit box key? The one Tilda somehow had? Yes, I think it is." Eliza stepped into the room, keeping distance between them. "She didn't destroy your business because of a recipe, did she? She did it because your husband was embezzling from his company—Tilda's late husband's company. And when you found out and threatened to expose him, he tried to poison you. But you switched the cups, didn't you? He died instead."

Marina's face crumbled completely, years falling away until she looked young and terrified. "It was self-defense. He was going to kill me and run away with her—with Tilda. They'd been having an affair for years. She provided the poison. I just... made sure he drank it instead of me."

"And you came back to Ashford Creek to what? Kill her the same way?"

"No!" Marina protested, tears flowing freely now. "I came back to see her exposed. That letter promised she'd finally pay for her crimes. I wanted to watch her fall. I wanted to see her face when everyone knew what she really was."

"Then who killed her?"

Before Marina could answer, footsteps thundered up both staircases. They were trapped between Wade's deputies coming up the front and someone else on the service stairs.

But as Wade and his deputies burst in from both doors, Eliza noticed something that made her stomach drop. Bruno was growling at the window—the one that overlooked the inn's Kitchen garden.

Down below, barely visible through the rain, a figure in a dark raincoat was burying something beneath the rosebushes. The figure was too far away to identify clearly, but something about the movement was familiar—controlled, efficient, military.

"Wade," Eliza said urgently. "The real killer is still here."

CHAPTER 5

BITTER TRUTHS

*W*ade sent Deputy Morris racing down to the garden while Marina was cuffed and led away. Morris, despite being in his fifties with a bad knee from his high school football days, moved with surprising speed when motivated. The rest of them watched from the parlor window as he disappeared into the rain, which had intensified to near-horizontal sheets.

The inn's garden, usually Millie's pride and joy, looked like a crime scene from a gothic novel. The heritage roses were beaten down, their pink and yellow blooms scattered like confetti at a funeral. The herb garden's neat borders had dissolved into mud. And there, near the oldest rosebush—a climber that had been planted when the inn was built—the earth was clearly disturbed.

"He's gone," Morris's voice crackled over Wade's radio. "But Sheriff, you need to see this."

By the time they reached the rosebushes, Morris had already begun excavating, his hands gentle despite the urgency. The rain had plastered his uniform to his body, making him look like a drowned scarecrow. He'd found a bundle wrapped in Kitchen plastic—the heavy-duty kind Millie used for storing holiday decorations.

"Don't touch it directly," Wade warned, pulling on fresh gloves.

Inside was an apron—one of the inn's, with "Teacup Inn" embroidered on the front in Millie's grandmother's distinctive script. The fabric was stained with white crystalline residue that the rain hadn't managed to wash away. Even from a distance, Eliza could smell it—bitter almonds, faint but unmistakable.

"Cyanide," Wade said grimly after a careful sniff. He sealed the apron in an evidence bag, rain pattering against the plastic. "Someone was covering their tracks."

They trudged back inside, a procession of soaked and shaken people. The inn felt different now—no longer a cozy refuge but a place where someone had methodically planned and executed murder. The tourists had been allowed to leave with strict instructions to remain available, but the locals were required to stay.

They were back in the tea room now, the afternoon growing dark as the storm intensified. The power had flickered twice already, and Millie had lit candles on each table, giving the room an inappropriately romantic atmosphere for a murder investigation. The dancing shadows made everyone look suspicious, faces shifting between light and dark like their secrets.

Marina sat in custody at a corner table, her expensive clothes now rumpled, her perfect makeup smeared. Deputy Lang sat across from her, ostensibly guarding but really just looking uncomfortable. Marina had been determined a flight risk but not yet formally arrested for Tilda's murder—

multiple witnesses confirmed she'd never left the main tea room until after Tilda's death. Her wet footprints on the back stairs proved she'd returned to search, not to kill.

"The apron changes things," Eliza said to Wade quietly, standing near the Kitchen door where they could observe everyone. "Whoever wore it had access to the Kitchen, knew about the poison, and was in the parlor."

"That's half the people here," Wade pointed out, frustration creeping into his usually steady voice. "All the staff, plus anyone who's been a regular. The inn's not exactly Fort Knox. Millie's never turned anyone away from her Kitchen."

As if to prove his point, Mrs. Henderson had wandered behind the counter to help herself to more hot water, moving with the confidence of someone who'd done it a hundred times before.

Bruno, who'd been sniffing around the room in an ever-widening pattern, suddenly stopped at Owens feet and sat. His old police signal for alerting to evidence. His tail was still, ears forward, completely focused.

Owen looked down, expression neutral as always, but Eliza caught the slight tension in his shoulders. "Smart dog."

"He is," Eliza agreed, keeping her voice conversational. "What's he smelling, Owen?"

Owen lifted his shoe—a practical work boot, worn but well-maintained. A white crystal was embedded in the tread, glinting in the candlelight. "Sugar," he said, voice flat. "From this morning's prep. Unless you think it's something else?"

The room had gone quiet, everyone watching. The candle-light made the crystal look like a tiny star against the dark rubber sole.

Wade bagged the shoe immediately, his movements effi-cient but somehow ominous. "We'll test it."

Owen surrendered it without protest, oddly calm for someone who'd just become a prime suspect. He stood in his sock feet, toes visible through a hole he probably hadn't known about. The small vulnerability made him seem more human, less like the controlled military machine he usually projected.

"Where were you when Tilda died?" Wade asked, pulling out his notebook.

"Kitchen, prepping for lunch. Charlie can confirm—he was in and out."

"Actually," Charlie said miserably from his corner table, his voice small in the large room, "you left for about ten minutes. Said you needed air. That was right before I went up with the tea."

Owen's calm finally cracked, just a hairline fracture but visible. His hands clenched and unclenched at his sides. "I stepped out back for a smoke. Is that a Crime?"

"Depends what you were smoking," Wade said evenly.

The tension ratcheted higher, the air thick enough to cut. Eliza watched the dynamics shift—people edging away from Owen, suspicious glances, whispered speculation. But something felt wrong. Too neat. Too obvious. Like someone was painting by numbers, and Owen was meant to be colored guilty.

"Millie," she said suddenly, an idea forming. "You said the spare key to the service door went missing. When did you notice?"

Millie thought, absently straightening silverware that didn't need straightening. "Monday? No, Sunday. After church service. We had Judge Morrison's anniversary tea, and I went to get the key to lock up, but it wasn't on the hook."

"Who was here Sunday?"

"Everyone," Millie said helplessly, gesturing at the room. "We had forty people for the anniversary, and the Kitchen was chaos. Anyone could have taken it."

Dr. Pemberton cleared his throat, the sound sharp in the tense atmosphere. He'd been so quiet that everyone had almost forgotten him, hidden in his corner like a turtle in its shell. "I may have seen something relevant." All eyes turned to him. He adjusted his glasses—a nervous habit Eliza had been counting. This was adjustment number forty-three since the investigation began. "Sunday afternoon, I saw Tilda leaving the inn through the back entrance—the staff entrance. She looked... furtive."

"Why didn't you mention this earlier?" Wade demanded, his patience finally fraying.

"I didn't think it relevant until now. But if she took the key..."

"She could have planted the poison herself," Patsy finished eagerly, practically bouncing in her seat. "Set someone up to take the fall."

"But why would she poison herself?" Rebecca Harris asked. Her voice was steady, but her hands weren't—they kept moving to her grandmother's ring, twist, twist, twist.

"She wouldn't," Eliza said, pieces clicking together in her mind. "Not intentionally. Which means—"

The lights went out completely.

Several people screamed. A chair crashed over—the sound explosive in the darkness. In the chaos, Eliza heard rapid footsteps, a door slamming, breaking glass from somewhere upstairs.

"Everyone stay still!" Wade shouted, his voice cutting through the panic.

Emergency lighting flickered on, casting eerie shadows

that made everyone look like suspects in a German expressionist film. The Henderson sisters were clutching each other, their faces pale as moonlight. Tom Garrett had knocked over his chair and stood frozen, half-crouched like he didn't know whether to run or hide. Charlie was pressed against the wall, eyes wide, breathing too fast.

And Owen was gone.

"The Kitchen," Wade barked, already moving.

They found the back door hanging open, rain driving in like an accusation. The wind had scattered papers from the counter, creating a snow of receipts and order tickets. Owen's remaining shoe sat abandoned on the threshold, looking somehow sadder than a pair would have.

But more concerning was what they found on the Kitchen counter: Millie's recipe box, forced open, its tiny lock twisted beyond repair. Papers were scattered everywhere—decades of carefully preserved family recipes spread like secrets across the stainless steel.

"No," Millie gasped, rushing to gather them. Her hands shook as she sorted through the papers, some so old the ink had faded to brown. "These are grandmother's recipes. They're irreplaceable—" She stopped, face paling to match the papers. "The lemon scone recipe. It's gone."

"But you said it was in the bank," Eliza said, confused.

Millie's face flushed. "I... I took it out yesterday. After Tilda's threats, I wanted to make sure it was really mine, that grandmother's notes were authentic. I was going to put it back today, but then..." She gestured helplessly at the chaos around them. "I never thought anyone would break into my personal recipe box. It's been in my family for seventy years."

"Owen took it?" Charlie asked, confused. "Why would he—"

"Why would Owen care about—" Eliza started, then stopped. Because there, caught on a splinter of the broken recipe box, was a torn piece of paper. She recognized Tilda's handwriting immediately—the same sharp angles, the same aggressive periods:

O.K. — Thursday, 11 a.m. Bring the proof about M.H. or I tell everyone about Fort Bragg.

"O.K.," Wade read. "Owen Kraft."

"M.H.," Millie whispered, her hand going to her throat. "That's me. Millicent Hart."

Eliza's mind raced, connections forming like a spider's web. "Tilda wasn't just threatening people randomly. She was collecting meetings. Marina said Tilda was meeting someone. This note proves it was Owen. But what proof about Millie?"

"I don't understand," Millie said tearfully. "What could Owen know about me? He's been nothing but loyal for three years. I gave him a chance when no one else would—"

Before anyone could answer, Bruno began barking urgently at the pantry door. Not his alert bark—his warning bark. The deep, aggressive sound he only made when there was immediate danger. Someone was in there.

CHAPTER 6

THE LOCKET IN THE GARDEN

*W*ade drew his service weapon—a Glock he'd carried for fifteen years, the metal worn smooth where his palm rested. "Police! Come out slowly!"

The door creaked open like a scene from a horror movie. Owen emerged, hands raised—but he wasn't alone. He was supporting someone, someone who'd been hidden in the pantry all along, someone small and shaking.

It was a young woman, maybe twenty-five, with Owen's same dark eyes and stubborn jaw. But where Owen was solid and controlled, she looked fragile, days of hiding written in the hollows of her cheeks and the tremor in her hands. Her clothes were wrinkled, her dark hair tangled, and she smelled of the mustiness that came from hiding in small spaces.

"My daughter," Owen said quietly, his voice holding a defeat Eliza had never heard from him. "Sarah. She's been living in the crawlspace under the inn for three days."

The room exploded in shocked voices, but Wade silenced them with a gesture. "Explain. Now."

Owen's shoulders sagged, the military bearing finally failing. "Sarah was at Fort Bragg with me. She was the real whistleblower—reported command for embezzlement. A major was skimming from the mess hall budget, selling supplies on the black market. Sarah had documented everything, had proof. But they flipped it, made it look like we were the thieves."

Sarah spoke for the first time, her voice hoarse from disuse. "Dad took the dishonorable discharge to protect me. Said he did it alone. But they still came after me—trumped up charges, threats. I've been running ever since."

"And Tilda found out," Eliza said, understanding dawning.

"She saw Sarah sneaking in Sunday night," Owen confirmed, his arm tightening protectively around his daughter. "The crawlspace has an old access from when they did the plumbing in the fifties. Sarah knew about it from when I showed her the inn's layout—habit from the military, always know your exits. Tilda threatened to call the MPs unless I helped her."

"Helped her how?" Wade asked, though his expression had softened slightly. He had a daughter too, away at college.

"She wanted dirt on Millie—specifically, proof that Millie's grandmother stole the lemon scone recipe from Tilda's family fifty years ago."

Millie gasped, her hand flying to her heart. "That's a lie! Grandmother created that recipe! She won awards—"

"I know," Owen said firmly. "But Tilda had forged documents, fake letters. She'd been building this false narrative for years. She was going to present them today unless I gave her real proof—proof I didn't have because it doesn't exist."

"So you poisoned her?" Wade asked, though doubt had crept into his voice.

"No!" Sarah spoke with surprising force for someone so

fragile-looking. "Dad would never. He was going to run, take me with him. We were packing when we heard the scream."

"Then who—" Wade started.

"Wait," Eliza interrupted, a crucial detail clicking. "Sarah, you've been hiding here three days. You must have seen things, heard things."

Sarah nodded slowly, her eyes darting nervously around the room. "Yesterday, I heard Tilda on the phone. She was in the parlor—the sound carries through the old radiator pipes. She said, 'I know what you did to Martha Harris twenty years ago. Bring fifty thousand to the parlor Thursday or everyone knows.'"

Rebecca Harris went white as bone. The ring she'd been twisting slipped off her finger and rang against the floor like a bell. "Martha was Charlie's aunt. She died in a car accident twenty years ago."

"It wasn't an accident," Charlie said suddenly, voice hollow. Everyone turned to stare at him. His face had taken on a gray cast, like old newspaper. "I found out last year. Went through Mom's old letters when I was looking for family recipes for a school project. Martha was having an affair with someone prominent. She threatened to go public. The accident... the brake lines were cut."

"Charlie," Rebecca breathed, reaching for her son. "Why didn't you tell me?"

"Because the letters implicated you, Mom!" Charlie's voice cracked like he was thirteen again. "They made it sound like you knew, like you helped cover it up to protect the family reputation. I couldn't—I couldn't ask you if you were—"

"A murderer," Rebecca finished, her voice barely a whisper. She sank into a chair like her strings had been cut. "I didn't know. I suspected, but I never knew for sure. And I never,

ever would have hurt Martha. She was my best friend before she was my sister-in-law."

"But Tilda thought you did," Eliza said, pieces clicking with terrible clarity. "She was blackmailing you too."

"She was blackmailing everyone," Patsy said bitterly, her usual composure completely gone. "Tom about watered-down medications. The Hendersons about selling forgeries. Dr. Pemberton about—"

"Enough," Pemberton said sharply, but his voice shook. "Yes, she had dirt on all of us. That's what she did—collected secrets like weapons."

Wade looked overwhelmed, running his hand through his hair in a gesture Eliza had seen when cases got too complex. "So everyone had motive."

"But not everyone had opportunity," Eliza pointed out. "Let's think about this. The poison was in a sugar jar—but which jar? Charlie, you said there were two?"

Charlie nodded miserably. "Tilda's, and the one already on the tea service."

"Who prepared the tea service?"

"I did," Owen said. "Early this morning, around six. Set it all up in the parlor."

"And I checked it," Millie added. "Around nine. Everything was perfect—wait." Her face changed, memory dawning. "The sugar jar was full. I noted it specifically because we'd been running low. I thought Owen had filled it."

"I didn't," Owen said with certainty. "I left it empty, planning to fill it later."

"But you didn't fill it?"

"No, I assumed someone else had."

Eliza felt the truth hovering just out of reach, like a word on the tip of her tongue. "So someone filled it between nine and when Charlie served the tea. Someone who knew Tilda would use the sugar, not her own."

"But Tilda insisted on her own jar," Charlie protested.

"Did she?" Eliza asked. "Or did she just insist on her special sugar being used? Charlie, think carefully. What exactly did she say?"

Charlie's brow furrowed in concentration. The candles flickered, making shadows dance across his face. "She said... she said 'Make sure to use the special sugar on my scone. It's already up there.'"

"Already up there," Eliza repeated. "She thought her jar was already in the parlor. Someone had switched them."

"But who?" Wade demanded.

Bruno had been sniffing around the group, and now he sat again—this time at Rebecca's feet. But he wasn't alerting. He was comforting, the way he did with victims, not perpetrators. His tail wagged once, gently, and he leaned against her leg.

And suddenly, Eliza knew.

"Charlie," she said gently. "You didn't go up the front stairs with the tea, did you? You used the service stairs. That's why the door was open."

Charlie went very still, like a rabbit sensing a hawk.

"You had the missing key," Eliza continued, her voice soft but inexorable. "You took it Sunday to get into the parlor. You knew about Tilda's plan to bring poisoned sugar—you'd overheard her on the phone, planning to frame someone for attempted murder. But you switched the jars. Put her poison in the house jar, left an empty one for her to bring."

"That's insane," Charlie said, but his voice shook like leaves in a storm.

"You knew she'd use the sugar already there if she thought

it was hers. She was arrogant that way. And you knew she was going to destroy your mother with those accusations about Martha Harris. You couldn't let that happen."

"Charlie?" Rebecca stared at her son in horror. "Is this true?"

Charlie's composure finally shattered like the china in the parlor. Tears streamed down his face, and his whole body shook with suppressed sobs. "She was evil!" he burst out. "She destroyed everything she touched! Marina's life, Owen's career, and she was going to destroy you, Mom. Make everyone think you were a murderer!"

"So you became one instead?" Wade asked quietly.

"I didn't mean for her to die!" Charlie sobbed, his words coming in rushes between gasping breaths. "I thought—I thought she'd just get sick. Scare her, make her back off. I didn't know how much poison she'd brought. I didn't know it would kill her so fast."

"You were trying to protect everyone," Eliza said. "But Charlie, you also wrote the threatening message in the pantry, didn't you? To throw suspicion elsewhere?"

He nodded miserably, looking younger than his nineteen years. "I panicked. I'm sorry. I'm so sorry."

Rebecca pulled her son into her arms, both of them crying now. The room stood in stunned silence, the only sound the rain against windows and the soft sobbing of mother and son.

Wade looked older suddenly, the weight of the situation visible in the lines of his face. "Charlie Harris, you're under arrest for the murder of Tilda Crane."

"No!" Rebecca cried out, her composure finally shattering completely. "This is all my fault! All of it!" She stumbled backward toward the stairs, sobbing.

"Rebecca, wait—" Wade started, but he had to secure

Charlie first. His hand moved to his belt, fingers finding the familiar metal of his handcuffs. But as he unclipped them, the lights went out again. This time, they heard a crash from upstairs—from the parlor.

Several people screamed. A chair crashed over in the darkness. Eliza heard rapid footsteps, a door slamming, glass breaking somewhere.

"Everyone stay still!" Wade shouted, his voice cutting through the panic.

They stood frozen in the darkness for what felt like an eternity but was probably only three or four minutes. The sound of rain against windows mixed with heavy breathing and someone's muffled sobbing. Wade's flashlight finally clicked on, sweeping the room.

"Stay here," Wade ordered, but Eliza was already moving, Bruno beside her.

They reached the parlor to find the window broken, rain driving in like an accusation. The curtains whipped in the wind like ghosts. Tilda's body remained in the chair, but something was different. A piece of paper was pinned to her chest—a paper that hadn't been there before.

Eliza read it by flashlight, her blood running cold:

Wrong killer. The boy's protecting someone. The real murder happened twenty years ago. Martha Harris didn't die in a car accident. She was murdered. And her killer just confessed.

"Eliza!" Wade's voice from below, urgent and shocked. "Rebecca's gone!"

They found her in the garden, kneeling in the rain where the apron had been buried. She was soaked through, her neat appearance destroyed, but she seemed calm. In her hands, she held a second bundle—this one wrapped in oilcloth, preserved for two decades.

"I kept it," she said numbly as they approached, rain mixing with tears on her face. "All these years, I kept the evidence. Because I thought someday I'd be brave enough to use it."

Wade knelt beside her, gently taking the bundle. Inside was a brake line, clearly cut, and a note in Tilda's younger handwriting: This should solve your Martha problem. You owe me.

"But I never asked her to," Rebecca said, her voice breaking completely. "Martha was going to leave town, start over. She wasn't going to expose anyone. But Tilda... Tilda thought she was doing me a favor. Protecting the family reputation. She killed Martha and expected me to be grateful."

"You've been living with this for twenty years," Eliza said softly, rain plastering her hair to her head.

"And Tilda held it over me the whole time. Not blackmail, exactly. Just... reminders. Little comments. 'Remember what I did for you.' 'Family loyalty is so important.' Until this week, when she finally demanded payment." Rebecca looked at her son, who had followed them out, Wade's cuffs still dangling from his wrist. "That's why I brought this evidence today—I was finally going to confront her at the meeting tonight. Charlie must have overheard more than I thought. He knew my plans. He tried to protect me by..." She broke down completely.

The rain had become a deluge, turning the garden into a mudscape that seemed appropriate for the unearthing of old secrets. The heritage roses, Millie's pride and usually standing tall even in storms, were beaten down, their petals scattered like confetti at a funeral no one wanted to attend. The smell of wet earth mixed with the lingering scent of roses created an oddly funereal perfume, sweet decay and fresh rain mingling into something that would forever remind Eliza of this moment.

Rebecca knelt in the mud, her neat appearance completely destroyed. Her usually perfect hair hung in wet strings, her makeup had run in dark rivers down her cheeks, and her clothes were soaked through. But there was something almost peaceful in her expression, as if confession had lifted a weight she'd carried so long she'd forgotten what it felt like to stand straight.

The evidence in her hands was wrapped with the kind of care usually reserved for holy relics. The oilcloth was old but well-maintained, the kind that might have wrapped fishing gear or hunting supplies two decades ago. Inside, the brake line was corroded but clearly cut—the edges too clean to be anything but deliberate. The note, protected by a plastic bag that had gone yellow with age, was still readable despite the years.

"I found them in my husband's things after he died," Rebecca said, her voice steady now that the worst was out. "He'd been having an affair with Martha—his own brother's wife. She was going to tell me, that's why she called that night. Said she had something important to discuss, something that couldn't wait. But she never made it."

Charlie stood beside his mother, the rain plastering his hair to his head, is face stripped of any pretense of adulthood. The expression on his face was something Eliza recognized from her years in Portland—the look of someone recalculating everything they thought they knew about their world. Every memory was being reexamined, every family story reevaluated in the harsh light of this new truth. His father had betrayed not just his mother, but his uncle too—a double betrayal that made the family gatherings, the shared holidays, all of it a lie.

"Tilda called me the next day," Rebecca continued. "Said she was sorry for my loss, but that Martha had been troubled, unstable. That the accident was probably for the best, that some secrets should die with the people who carry them. I knew then. The way she said it, the satisfaction in her voice. She'd done something. But I was a coward. I had Charlie to think about, a business to run, my brother-in-law who'd just lost his wife, a life to maintain. So I kept quiet and kept the evidence, telling myself that someday I'd be brave enough to use it."

Eliza had been studying Rebecca throughout her confession, and now she noticed something that made her step closer. "Rebecca, you have something on your face."

Rebecca touched her cheek, confused. Her fingers came away with a black smudge—the kind that came from permanent marker. More telling, there was a matching streak of black on her palm, and when she'd touched her face, she'd transferred it. The same deep black as the writing on the note pinned to Tilda's body.

"You wrote the note during the blackout," Eliza said quietly. "With a marker from the parlor desk."

Rebecca's shoulders sagged in defeat. "When the lights went out," she continued, her voice hollow, "I knew Charlie was about to be arrested for something I'd caused. I couldn't let that happen. I slipped upstairs in the darkness—I know this inn like my own home, every creaking board. I found the marker in the desk drawer and wrote that note, then pinned it to her. I wanted everyone to know the real murder was Martha's, twenty years ago. I wanted them to know my boy was just trying to protect me from the truth." She looked at Wade. "I'm sorry for tampering with the scene. But I couldn't let Charlie take the blame alone."

Wade's expression was unreadable. "You wrote the note during the blackout?"

"Yes. I had to make sure everyone knew there was more to this. That the real crime happened twenty years ago."

Wade stood in the rain, looking between mother and son, the weight of Solomon on his shoulders. "So Charlie poisoned Tilda to stop her from revealing that Tilda herself was a murderer?"

"The irony," Dr. Pemberton said from the doorway, having ignored Wade's order to stay put, "is that Tilda finally got justice. Just not the kind she expected."

"There's no justice in any of this," Wade said heavily. "Just tragedy all the way down, like Russian nesting dolls of pain."

But as they stood in the garden, rain washing away twenty years of secrets, Eliza noticed something that changed everything.

Bruno was alerting again—but not to any person. He was focused on the rosebush itself, nose pointing like an arrow at the base where something metallic gleamed among the roots. His tail was rigid, his whole body tense with discovery.

The metallic gleam in the rosebush turned out to be a small silver locket, tarnished with age but still intact. Wade extracted it carefully with gloved hands, the rain making everything slippery and difficult. The locket was heart-shaped, Victorian in style, with delicate etching that had survived two decades in the earth.

Bruno sat perfectly still, his alert posture rigid despite the rain soaking through his coat. His training held even in the storm—once he'd indicated evidence, he wouldn't move until released. Eliza gave him the command to relax, and he shook himself, sending water everywhere, but his eyes remained fixed on Wade's hands.

"Let me see," Rebecca said, reaching with trembling fingers.

Wade opened the locket with careful pressure. The hinge protested but held. Inside was a photograph, protected by glass that had somehow remained uncracked. Two young women smiled at the camera—one clearly Martha Harris, young and vibrant with eyes that matched Charlie's. The other face had been carefully cut out with surgical precision, leaving a perfect oval void.

"That's Martha's locket," Rebecca said, her voice hollow with shock. "She was wearing it when she died. She never took it off—it was her grandmother's. How did it get here?"

CHAPTER 7

THE LAST CUP

*T*he question hung in the air like the rain, persistent and unanswerable. The locket shouldn't exist. It should have been destroyed in the accident, or buried with Martha, or at the very least, lost to time. Its presence here, in Millie's rose garden, suggested something far more complex than they'd imagined.

"Someone saved it," Eliza said slowly, her detective mind working through possibilities. "Someone was at the accident scene. Someone who knew what really happened."

"But the police report—" Wade started.

"Could have been altered. We already know Tilda had connections, money to throw around." Eliza studied the locket, noting the careful way the photo had been cut. "This wasn't random. Someone wanted to preserve Martha's image but eliminate the other person."

They stood in the rain, a bedraggled group of suspects and investigators, all soaked through and shivering. The storm had turned cold, more like October than late spring, and

Charlie was shaking so hard his teeth chattered. Rebecca had her arm around him, but she looked ready to collapse herself.

"Everyone inside," Wade commanded. "We're solving this tonight, but not if half of you die of pneumonia."

They trooped back into the inn, leaving puddles in their wake. Millie immediately began distributing towels she'd gathered, her innkeeper instincts overriding the surreal situation. The tea room felt different now—charged with the weight of revealed secrets and the promise of more to come. The candles had burned lower, creating pools of wax that looked like frozen tears.

Charlie sat with Deputy Morris, having confessed but not yet formally arrested. The handcuffs remained off, a small mercy from Wade who seemed to be weighing justice against tragedy with every decision. Rebecca stayed close to her son, mother and son bound by their mutual desire to protect each other and their shared guilt over actions taken and not taken.

Sarah and Owen huddled near the Kitchen, her exhaustion evident in every line of her body. Three days of hiding in crawlspaces had taken their toll—she looked like she might collapse at any moment. Owen kept a protective arm around her, but his own strength was flagging. The soldier's bearing that had kept him upright through everything was finally failing.

Marina sat alone at her table, guarded by Deputy Lang who looked increasingly uncomfortable with his job. She'd stopped crying, but her face held a bleakness that was worse than tears.

"We need to piece this together properly," Wade said, exhaustion clear in his voice. He'd been sheriff for fifteen years, but nothing had prepared him for this—a murder with three potential killers and a victim who was herself a murderer. "Charlie, tell us exactly what you did. Every detail."

Charlie wiped his eyes with the towel Millie had given him. When he spoke, his voice was thin but steady, like he'd moved past panic into a numb acceptance. "Sunday night, I couldn't sleep. I kept thinking about what Tilda had said to Mom at the grocery store—these hints about Martha, about family secrets. So I went for a walk around two AM. I saw Tilda's car at the inn, which was weird."

"The inn was closed," Millie said, frowning.

"That's what I thought. So I used my key and came in the back way. I heard voices from upstairs—Tilda was on the phone in the parlor. The acoustics in this old place are weird; if you stand in the right spot in the Kitchen, you can hear everything from the parlor through the radiator pipes."

Sarah nodded confirmation. "It's true. I heard things too."

Charlie continued, his hands twisting the towel. "She was talking about bringing 'special sugar' to her Thursday meeting teach someone a lesson. She said something about frame insurance, about making sure she couldn't be blamed. I thought she was going to poison someone today and make it look like an accident or frame them for attempted murder."

"So you decided to beat her to it," Wade said.

"I panicked. I took the service key from the hook—I knew where Millie kept it. This morning, really early, like five AM, I went up to the parlor. I was just going to check, you know? See if she'd left anything. But then I found this note." Charlie pulled a crumpled paper from his pocket—another piece of evidence he'd hidden. Wade took it, read it, and his expression darkened further.

The note was in block printing, not Tilda's handwriting:

"For Tilda—Your special sugar is already in place. Use it generously. Justice is patient but not indefinite. —M.C."

"M.C.," Eliza breathed, then paused. "Wait. What was Martha Harris's maiden name?"

Rebecca looked up, confused by the question. "Caldwell. Martha Caldwell. She kept her maiden name professionally even after marrying my brother."

"M.C.," Wade said slowly. "Martha Caldwell."

"But that's impossible," Rebecca said. "Martha's been dead for twenty years."

"Or someone wants us to think she sent it," Wade said. "Charlie, what did you do when you found this note?"

Charlie's face crumpled. "I thought someone else was planning to poison Tilda. So I... I went to her usual table in the tea room. She always sat at the same place for her morning meetings, had for years. There was a small jar there, crystal with a silver lid, just like the ones we use for the private parlor. I thought it was Tilda's poison."

"But it wasn't," Eliza said, understanding dawning.

"I took it and put it in the house sugar jar in the parlor. I figured if she was planning to poison someone, she deserved to get a taste of her own medicine. Not to kill her!" His voice cracked. "Just to make her sick, scare her, make her back off from Mom."

"But you put cyanide in the jar," Wade said.

"I didn't know it was cyanide! I thought it was something milder, something to cause stomach upset maybe. Like ipecac or something. I never meant—" He broke off, sobbing again.

Eliza had been thinking, and something didn't add up. "Charlie, you said you took sugar from Tilda's usual table. But Tilda brought her jar with her this morning. So whose sugar did you actually take?"

Charlie went pale. "I... I don't know."

"Someone else planted poison," Eliza said. "Before you, before Tilda. Someone who knew exactly what would happen." She turned to the room. "Someone who's been planning revenge for twenty years."

Sarah Kraft, who'd been silent in her corner, suddenly spoke. Her voice was stronger now, as if telling the truth had given her energy. "There's something else. When I was hiding in the crawlspace, I found old blueprints. Original ones from when the inn was built. There's a sealed room in the basement that's not on any current floor plan."

Millie gasped, her hand flying to her throat. "Grandmother always said there were secrets in the foundation, but I thought she meant metaphorically."

"Show us," Wade ordered.

They descended into the basement, a procession of suspects and investigators. The basement was exactly what you'd expect in a Victorian inn—stone foundation, wooden beam ceiling, the musty smell of age and damp. Sarah led them past the modern utilities to what appeared to be a solid wall. But Bruno immediately began pawing at one corner, his nose working furiously.

"Here," Sarah said, running her hands along the wall. "There's a seam."

Owen produced a crowbar from the utility closet—he knew where everything was in this inn, three years of working here evident in every movement. The paint had sealed the edges, decades of layers creating a barrier. It took effort, Owen and Wade working together, before the hidden door finally gave way with a groan that sounded almost human.

The door opened to reveal a small room, musty with age

but surprisingly dry. A single bulb hung from the ceiling—someone had wired it recently, the electrical work modern. Inside was a desk, covered in papers, photographs, and newspaper clippings—all about Martha Harris's death.

But more shocking was what sat in the corner: a bed, recently slept in, with a neat stack of clothes beside it. Someone had been living here.

"Someone's been staying in the inn," Millie whispered, horrified. "In my own basement."

The walls were covered with surveillance—photos of Tilda taken from various angles over what looked like years. Tilda at the grocery store. Tilda at town meetings. Tilda at the inn. Some were date-stamped going back five years. Others were as recent as yesterday.

Eliza examined the papers on the desk. They were detailed notes about everyone in Ashford Creek—their routines, their secrets, their vulnerabilities. Tilda featured prominently, with twenty years of observations. Every cruel thing she'd done was documented, every person she'd hurt catalogued.

The most recent entry was from yesterday: Tomorrow, it ends where it began.

"This is..." Wade picked up a photograph. It showed the tea service in the parlor, with a clear shot of someone adding something to the sugar jar. The timestamp was 4:47 AM—before Charlie's visit.

"So Charlie really did poison Tilda," Rebecca said, her voice hollow, "but with poison someone else planted, expecting Tilda to serve it to someone else."

"The question is who," Wade said.

Bruno had moved to the bed, sniffing intently. He pawed at the pillow, and something crinkled. Eliza lifted it to find an envelope addressed to "The Truth Seekers of Ashford Creek."

Inside was a confession, but not the one they expected. Eliza read it aloud, her voice steady despite the shock:

My name is Margaret Caldwell—Martha's younger sister. Everyone thinks I died in foster care after Martha's death and our parents' deportation. But I survived. I changed my name, my face, my entire identity. I became Marina Blackwood, among others.

For twenty years, I've waited. I knew Tilda killed my sister. I knew Rebecca suspected but did nothing. I knew this entire town chose comfortable lies over justice for an orphaned immigrant girl.

I came back for the antique fair because I knew Tilda would be at her most vulnerable—her reputation on the line, her control slipping. I planted the cyanide, knowing her patterns, knowing she always tested her "special ingredients" herself first. But I wanted her to know why she was dying. I wanted her to see Martha's face in mine.

The boy complicated things by switching the jars, but the result was the same. Tilda Crane is dead by the poison she so loved to metaphorically spread. Justice is served.

I'll be gone by the time you read this. Don't look for Margaret Harris or Marina Blackwood. Both are ghosts now.

But know this—Martha Harris mattered. Her life had value. And her death has finally been avenged.

"Marina is Martha's sister?" Patsy gasped from the doorway—the entire group had followed them down, unable to stay away.

"That's why she looked familiar," Millie said slowly. "She has Martha's eyes. The same shape, the same unusual green color."

Wade immediately radioed his deputies. "Find Marina Blackwood. Now."

But Eliza was studying the photograph of the sugar jar more carefully. The person in the image was partially reflected in an antique mirror on the parlor wall—distorted but clear enough. "Wade, look at this. The person adding the poison—you can see their reflection in the mirror."

Wade looked closer, pulling out his reading glasses. "That's not Marina."

The reflection was distorted but clear enough: a man's profile, familiar and unexpected. The distinctive nose, the way he held his shoulders, even the characteristic way he tilted his head when concentrating.

"Dr. Pemberton," Eliza said.

Everyone turned to where the doctor had been standing, but he was gone. His absence was like a shout in the sudden silence. They heard a car engine starting outside, tires squealing on wet pavement.

"He's running!" Charlie shouted.

Wade was already on his radio, calling in roadblocks. "All units, be on the lookout for Dr. Pemberton's blue Volvo, license plate—" He rattled off the number from memory, a small-town sheriff who knew every car in his jurisdiction.

Within minutes, word came back—Pemberton had been stopped at the town limits, caught at the very boundary between Ashford Creek and the outside world.

They brought him back to the inn in cuffs, a shocking sight for someone who'd been the town's respected physician for thirty years. He looked older, defeated, all his pompous authority drained away like water from a broken cup. His usually perfect hair was disheveled, his glasses askew, and his hands—surgeon's hands that had saved lives—shook with tremors.

"Why?" Wade asked simply.

Pemberton's laugh was bitter, broken. "Why? Because Tilda destroyed everything she touched. Martha Harris was my patient. She came to me, pregnant and scared, begging for help. The baby's father was prominent—a married man, someone important in town. It wouldn't do for a scandal. "Tilda convinced me to break confidentiality. Said it was for Martha's own good. Said the father had a right to know. I was young, stupid, believed in hierarchies and social order."

"You told the father," Eliza said quietly.

"I told Tilda who the father was, and she told him. He arranged the accident. Cut her brake lines. Martha died because I broke my oath, because I trusted Tilda Crane." Tears ran down his face, mixing with rain residue. "I've been drowning in that guilt for twenty years."

"So you decided to kill Tilda."

"When Margaret contacted me—yes, I knew who Marina really was—she didn't hide it from me. She said she had a plan for justice. I saw a chance for redemption." He looked at his cuffed hands. "I planted the first poison, the real poison, knowing Tilda's habits. She always came early on Thursdays to set up her power plays. She always tested anything she planned to serve, paranoid about her own tricks being turned on her."

"You've been living with this guilt for twenty years," Eliza said.

"Living with it? I've been drowning in it. Every patient I saved felt like penance that was never enough. When Margaret told me her plan, I saw a chance to finally balance the scales."

"You let Charlie think he was a murderer," Rebecca said, furious, mother's rage giving her strength.

"The boy was trying to protect you," Pemberton said.

"Noble, if misguided. He would have been charged with manslaughter at worst, probably gotten probation. Meanwhile, the real killer—Tilda's own arrogance—did her in."

"Except you're the real killer." Wade said. "You put the cyanide there."

"I put medicine there," Pemberton corrected with a ghost of his old precision. "Tilda turned it into poison by being herself."

The legal arguments would be complex, Eliza knew. Charlie had switched jars with intent to harm. Pemberton had planted the poison. Marina/Margaret had orchestrated it all. But ultimately, Tilda had insisted on using what she thought was her own weapon.

"Where is Marina now?" Wade asked Pemberton.

"Gone. She slipped away during all that confusion with the pantry. Her revenge was complete. Twenty years of planning for ten seconds of watching Tilda realize she'd been poisoned by her own weapon."

But Bruno was alerting again, this time at the kitchen door. When they opened it, Marina stood there, soaking wet, looking nothing like the composed woman from this morning. Her elegant clothes were plastered to her body, her makeup completely gone, revealing a face that looked younger and infinitely sadder.

"I couldn't leave," she said simply. "Not without visiting Martha's grave. Twenty years, and I never got to say goodbye to my sister properly. But standing there in the rain, I realized I couldn't run. Not again." As he read her rights, she looked at Rebecca. "You should have helped her. She trusted you."

"I know," Rebecca whispered. "I've lived with that failure every day."

"And you?" Marina looked at Charlie. "You have your

mother's protective instincts but also her weakness—the inability to act when it mattered most."

"That's enough," Wade said, leading her away.

But Marina turned back one more time. "I left something else in that room. Under the mattress. You should see it before you decide who's really guilty here."

Wade sent Deputy Morris to check. He returned with a manila folder—thick, worn, held together with rubber bands. Inside were documents, photos, evidence spanning twenty years.

"These are..." Wade's voice trailed off as he examined them.

The documents told a story of systematic cruelty that spanned decades. Each folder was meticulously labeled in Tilda's distinctive handwriting—names, dates, amounts. The Henderson sisters had been paying her five hundred dollars a month for three years to keep quiet about a forged Tiffany lamp they'd sold to a collector from Boston. Tom Garrett's payments were irregular but larger—sometimes two thousand, sometimes five, corresponding to shipments of medications that were approaching expiration but relabeled with fresh dates.

But it was the folder labeled "Martha Harris" that made everyone in the room step back. Inside were photographs— Martha with her lover, taken with a telephoto lens through bedroom windows. Bank statements showing deposits from him to her account. Medical records that should have been confidential, including the pregnancy test results. And at the bottom, a receipt from an auto parts store for brake line tools, dated three days before Martha's death, paid for with Tilda's credit card. She didn't just arrange Martha's death—she planned it for months."

"She documented her own crime," Wade said, disbelief clear in his voice. "Why would she keep this?"

"Insurance," Marina said quietly from her corner. "That's how she thought. Everyone was potentially an enemy, so she kept evidence on everyone, including herself. If someone tried to expose her, she could claim they were framing her, that they'd planted the evidence. She'd have revealed just enough to make herself look like a victim of an elaborate setup."

"There's more," Morris said, pulling out newer documents. "Tilda's been blackmailing half the town for decades. But look at this—she was embezzling from the town council, from the church, from every charity she ever ran."

Margaret pulled out another folder, this one labeled "Emergency Exit." Inside were plane tickets to the Cayman Islands, dated for Thursday afternoon. Bank routing numbers for offshore accounts. A new identity complete with passport and driver's license—Helen Crawford, a widow from Connecticut with no children and no ties.

"She was never going to reveal anything at the town meeting," Eliza said, understanding dawning. "She was going to disappear. Take everyone's money and run."

"But not before one final score," Wade said, pulling out a draft email on Tilda's personal stationary. It was addressed to the town council, scheduled to be sent Thursday morning: "Due to family emergency, I must leave immediately. I've left important documents in the town hall safe that must be reviewed by state authorities. The truth about Ashford Creek's corruption must come to light."

"She was going to frame everyone for her crimes," Dr. Pemberton said, his face pale. "Leave us to deal with the accusations while she vanished with the money."

The room stood in stunned silence as the full scope of

Tilda's plan became clear. She'd spent twenty years gathering weapons, and she'd planned to fire them all at once, leaving the town to destroy itself while she escaped to a new life built on their ruins.

"Then why bring poison?" Rebecca asked.

Eliza thought about it, pieces clicking. "Insurance. If someone tried to stop her, she'd poison them and claim self-defense. She'd done it before—there are three other deaths here over the years that look suspicious in hindsight."

The inn stood in shocked silence. Three killers, in a way—Marina who planned it, Pemberton who enabled it, and Charlie who executed it unknowingly. And at the center, Tilda herself, whose cruelty had sewn the seeds of her own destruction.

"What happens now?" Millie asked quietly.

Wade looked exhausted beyond measure. "Now we let the lawyers sort it out. Three people conspired to kill a woman who was also a murderer. I don't even know where to begin with the charges."

"Maybe," Eliza said quietly, "we begin with the truth. All of it. Let the town know who Tilda really was. Let them know about Martha. Let justice be served with full knowledge, not comfortable lies."

Thunder rumbled overhead, softer now, the storm finally passing. Through the windows, they could see breaks in the clouds, stars beginning to appear.

"It's Thursday," someone said. "The town meeting is in two hours."

Wade straightened his shoulders. "Then we'd better get ready to tell them everything."

* * *

THURSDAY EVENING ARRIVED with unexpected sunshine breaking through the clouds, as if nature itself wanted to witness Ashford Creek's reckoning. The Town Hall, a Greek Revival building that had served the community since 1853, was packed beyond capacity. People stood in the aisles, lined the walls, and spilled out onto the front steps where someone had set up speakers to broadcast the proceedings.

Wade stood at the podium where Tilda had planned to stand, still in his sheriff's uniform, still damp from the afternoon's rain. Beside him, a table held the evidence boxes, each one labeled and sealed, waiting to tell their part of the story.

"Folks," Wade began, his deep voice carrying even to those outside. "What I'm about to tell you isn't easy to hear. But after twenty years of secrets, this town deserves the truth."

He started with Martha Harris, projecting her photograph onto the screen behind him—young, smiling, full of life. "Martha Harris died twenty years ago in what we believed was an accident. It wasn't. She was murdered by Tilda Crane, who cut her brake lines because Martha was pregnant and threatening to expose an affair."

The gasps rippled through the crowd like wind through wheat. Mrs. Henderson clutched her sister's hand. Tom Garrett removed his glasses, cleaning them with shaking hands.

"But that was just the beginning," Wade continued. He detailed Tilda's twenty-year reign of blackmail, each revelation landing like a physical blow on the assembled crowd. The forged documents about Millie's grandmother's recipe. The false evidence she'd planted about various citizens. The money she'd extracted—nearly half a million dollars over two decades.

"She was planning to leave town," Wade said simply. "Take

your money and disappear, leaving you all to deal with the chaos she'd created."

The crowd erupted in voices—anger, relief, confusion mixing into a cacophony that Mayor Doyle had to gavel into order.

"The poison that killed her—she brought it herself," Wade continued once quiet returned. "She intended to use it on someone else. Instead, through a series of events I can only describe as poetic justice, she ingested it herself."

He explained the complicated web of Charlie's attempt to protect his mother, Dr. Pemberton's involvement, and Margaret Harris's twenty-year quest for justice. The crowd listened in stunned silence as the full story unfolded.

"Three people have been arrested," Wade said. "The district attorney will sort out the charges. But what matters now is what we do next."

He paused, looking out at the assembled faces—his neighbors, his community, the people he'd sworn to protect and serve. "We can let this destroy us, let suspicion and blame tear apart what's left of our community. Or we can choose to rebuild, to be honest with each other, to create the town we always pretended we were."

The silence stretched until Millie Hart stood up, still wearing her inn apron, her face tear-stained but determined. "I propose we start fresh. All of it. The secrets Tilda collected die with her. We support the Harris family, we forgive each other's mistakes, and we move forward. Together."

"But what about the money she stole?" someone called out.

"We'll work with the district attorney and file civil suits to recover the extorted funds," Mayor Doyle said, standing. "Her estate will go through probate, and we'll petition the court for restitution. It may take months, maybe longer, but we'll fight to get every penny back. And if there's anything left after victims are compensated, I propose we request it be used to create a memorial scholarship in Martha Harris's name."

Tom Garrett stood next, his pharmacist's coat still on. "I want to apologize. To all of you. I did things I'm not proud of to keep Tilda quiet. But no more. From now on, transparency. And seniors get a permanent discount at my pharmacy."

One by one, people stood. The Henderson sisters admitted their antique might indeed be a reproduction. Sally Brennan, the nurse practitioner who worked with Dr. Pemberton, announced she'd keep the practice open. "I've been here five years. I know all of you. We'll manage just fine."

Owen Kraft stood, glancing at Millie for permission before speaking. "If Millie agrees, the inn could host a free community dinner next Thursday—to remember that we're neighbors, not enemies."

Millie nodded immediately. "Of course we will. The inn was built to bring people together. It's time we remembered that."

By the time the meeting ended, something had shifted in Ashford Creek. The perfect facade had cracked, but what emerged wasn't ugliness—it was humanity. Flawed, complicated, but ultimately forgiving humanity.

As people filed out into the evening sunshine, Eliza heard snippets of conversation: "Can you believe Tilda was going to run?" "Poor Martha. All these years..." "Maybe we needed this. Maybe we needed the truth." And from Mrs. Henderson to her sister: "You know, I'm almost glad that armoire is fake. The insurance value was giving me ulcers." They laughed—actual, genuine laughter—and Eliza realized that Ashford Creek might actually emerge from this stronger than before.

EPILOGUE

SIX MONTHS LATER

*T*he Teacup Inn was quiet on a Thursday morning, exactly six months after Tilda Crane's death. Eliza sat at her usual table, Bruno dozing at her feet, writing in her notebook. She was documenting everything, not for publication but for clarity—her own need to understand how a town's silence had led to such tragedy.

The legal aftermath had been surprisingly merciful. The district attorney, faced with the complexity of the case and the public revelation of Tilda's crimes, had offered plea deals all around. Charlie received two years probation and community service—teaching cooking classes to underprivileged youth. Dr. Pemberton lost his medical license but avoided jail time due to his age and cooperation. Margaret Caldwell— she'd legally reclaimed her real name—was serving eighteen months in minimum security, with the possibility of early release.

The town had been shocked by the revelations at the emergency meeting. Learning that their social leader had been a murderer, blackmailer, and thief had shaken Ashford Creek to its foundation. But in typical small-town fashion, they were rebuilding, carefully, with more honesty than before.

"Your tea," Millie said, setting down the familiar cup. "And Owen's new lemon scones. He's calling them 'Truth Scones'—completely transparent recipe, no secrets."

Indeed, Owen had posted the recipe in the window for anyone to copy. The secret, it turned out, was not in hidden ingredients but in the technique—something that couldn't be stolen, only learned.

"Sarah?" Eliza asked. "How is she?"

"Thriving, actually. The military review board overturned her case thanks to all the publicity. She's officially cleared and working with Owen in the kitchen. They make a good team." Millie smiled. "She's even started dating Tom Garrett's son—the one who just graduated from UVM. The town really rallied around her once they knew the truth."

Charlie appeared in the doorway, broom in hand. His community service included helping at the inn, and he'd thrown himself into it with dedication. "Ms. Prescott, Bruno's treat?"

Bruno's tail thumped hopefully. Charlie had taken to bringing homemade dog biscuits, his way of making amends to everyone, even the dog who'd helped expose him.

"Thank you, Charlie," Eliza said, watching him carefully give Bruno the treat. "How are you doing?"

"Better," he said simply. "The kids at the community center don't know about... everything. To them, I'm just the guy who teaches them to make cookies. It's nice."

Rebecca arrived for her weekly visit with Charlie, and

Eliza watched mother and son embrace. They were healing, slowly, the kind of healing that comes from truth rather than comfortable lies.

Sheriff Wade entered, looking less exhausted than he had two weeks ago. "Morning, Eliza. Any new mysteries to solve?"

"Just the usual. Mrs. Henderson thinks someone's stealing her garden gnomes."

"Raccoons," Wade said immediately.

"That's what I told her. She wants a full investigation."

They shared a smile—normal problems, small-town concerns. It was refreshing after the intensity of Tilda's murder.

"You know," Wade said, settling into the chair across from her, "the town council wants to create an official position. Part-time investigator, help me with the complex cases. Interested?"

Eliza looked around the inn—at Millie humming as she served customers, at Owen and Sarah laughing in the Kitchen, at Charlie carefully sweeping the entrance. The town had survived its trial by poison. People were choosing honesty over comfortable lies, community over isolation.

"Ask me after I solve the gnome case," she said.

Bruno woofed in agreement, and Wade laughed—the first real laugh she'd heard from him since this all began.

Outside, the sun shone on Main Street, warming the cobblestones and bringing out the spring flowers. The Teacup Inn's windows gleamed, reflecting not the past but the possibility of the future.

In her notebook, Eliza wrote: Case closed. But in a town like Ashford Creek, there's always another secret waiting to surface. The difference now is that the town faces them together, with truth as their witness and tea as their comfort.

She closed the notebook and sipped her tea. It was perfect —no secrets, no poison, just the honest comfort of a well-made cup.

For now, that was enough.

MILLIE HART'S GRANDMOTHER'S LEMON SCONES

The recipe that started it all—finally revealed after 70 years

Makes 8 scones

"The secret was never about hiding ingredients. It was about technique, timing, and putting love into every batch. Grandmother would be happy to know it's finally being shared." —Millie Hart

Ingredients:

- 2 cups all-purpose flour
- 1/3 cup granulated sugar
- 1 tablespoon baking powder
- 1/2 teaspoon salt
- Zest of 2 large lemons
- 6 tablespoons cold unsalted butter, cut into small cubes
- 1/2 cup heavy cream (plus extra for brushing)
- 1 large egg
- 2 tablespoons fresh lemon juice

- 1 teaspoon vanilla extract

For the Signature Glaze:

- 1 cup powdered sugar
- 3 tablespoons fresh lemon juice
- 1 tablespoon heavy cream
- Pinch of salt
- Optional: 1/4 teaspoon almond extract (the safe kind!)

Instructions:

1. **Preheat and Prepare:** Heat your oven to 425°F. Line a baking sheet with parchment paper.
2. **The Secret First Step:** Place your mixing bowl and pastry cutter in the freezer for 10 minutes before starting. Cold tools make all the difference.
3. **Mix Dry Ingredients:** In your chilled bowl, whisk together flour, sugar, baking powder, salt, and lemon zest.
4. **Cut in the Butter:** Add cold butter cubes. Using a pastry cutter or two knives, cut butter into flour until mixture resembles coarse crumbs with some pea-sized pieces. Work quickly—the butter must stay cold.
5. **Combine Wet Ingredients:** In a separate bowl, whisk together cream, egg, lemon juice, and vanilla.
6. **The Gentle Fold:** Make a well in the center of flour mixture. Pour in wet ingredients. Using a fork,

gently stir until dough just comes together. Don't overmix—this is crucial!

7. **Shape with Care:** Turn dough onto lightly floured surface. Gently pat into a circle about 8 inches across and 3/4 inch thick. Cut into 8 wedges.

8. **The Final Touch:** Place wedges on prepared baking sheet, 2 inches apart. Brush tops with cream and sprinkle with a little sugar.

9. **Bake to Perfection:** Bake 15-17 minutes until golden brown on top and bottom.

10. **Glaze While Warm:** Mix all glaze ingredients until smooth. Drizzle over warm scones.

Millie's Tips:

- Never overwork the dough—gentle hands make tender scones
- The dough should be slightly sticky; resist adding too much flour
- For best results, serve within 2 hours of baking
- Store leftovers in airtight container for up to 2 days

OWEN'S TRUTH SCONES

A new recipe for a new beginning—no secrets, just good technique

Makes 8 scones

"After everything that happened, I wanted to create something honest. These scones have no secret ingredients—just good technique and quality materials.' —Owen Kraft

Ingredients:

- 2 cups all-purpose flour
- 1/4 cup sugar
- 2 teaspoons baking powder
- 1/2 teaspoon baking soda
- 1/2 teaspoon salt
- 1 stick (8 tablespoons) frozen butter
- 1/2 cup buttermilk
- 1 large egg
- 1 teaspoon vanilla
- Optional mix-ins: chocolate chips, dried cranberries, or fresh blueberries

Instructions:

1. **Heat oven to 400°F.** Line baking sheet with parchment.
2. **Grate the frozen butter** using a box grater—this is Owen's trick for perfect distribution without warming the butter.
3. **Mix flour, sugar, baking powder, baking soda, and salt** in large bowl.
4. **Add grated butter,** tossing with flour mixture to coat.
5. **Whisk buttermilk, egg, and vanilla** in small bowl.
6. **Combine wet and dry** until just mixed. Fold in any mix-ins.
7. **Pat dough** into 8-inch circle on floured surface. Cut into 8 wedges.
8. **Bake 18-20 minutes** until golden.

Owen's Note: "The frozen butter trick came from my army days—we had to get creative with field kitchens. Works every time."

ALSO BY ELLA ANDREW

The Agatha Royale Mystery Series

• One Deadly Chapter (Book 1)

• One Deadly Batch (Book 2)

• One Deadly Needle (Book 3)

• One Deadly Safari (Book 4)

• One Deadly Premier (Book 5 - Coming Soon)

The Ashford Creek Mysteries

Quick reads perfect for your lunch break or evening escape

• Death at the Teacup Inn (Book 1)

• Death at the Sweet Festival (Book 2 - Coming Soon)

Each Ashford Creek Mystery is a complete story you can enjoy in about 2 hours.

All books available on Amazon

Other works

Daughters of the Crescent Moon Series

Destiny's Past

Destiny's Present

Destiny's Future

Without a Paddle

Short stories about life's struggles

Patricia C. Lee

Phoenix Literary Publishing
phoenixlitpub@gmail.com

ISBN: 9780994851277
ISBN: 9780994851215

CONTENTS

A Holy Night

Dusk settled, quiet, solemn, bringing bittersweet memories in the fading light. Her hand shook, but arthritic fingers gnarled with times' passage held fast to the record player's plastic arm. The needle jumped, skittered over worn grooves, landing too far into the vinyl recording. She tried again, one hand cradling another, until the prelude's rewarding skip and crackle indicated the correct mark. Strains of music filtered from mismatched speakers.

She straightened her aged shoulders, aching and stooped from years of manual labor, and shuffled to the window. The routine, as ingrained as brushing her teeth, happened only once a year.

Tradition.

A puff of warm air dissipated intricate frost patterns on the window, the sweater's threadbare woolen sleeve removed a circle of winter's breath from the pane to reveal the snow-blanketed countryside and pine branches decorated like globs of icing. December's full moon radiated amid sparkling stars, basking the view in surreal luminescence. Her rheumy eyes scanned the yard, into the tree line beyond, searching, hoping, praying this would be the year he returned. Phosphorus raked against a matchbox side, fire flared, quieted, to light the single candle anchored into a holder on the sill.

A guide.

She turned, eyes traveling the room, taking in the assortment of antique decorations, their valiant effort for cheer lying buried beneath layers of dust. Pine cone wreath, its faded tartan ribbon arranged to cover gaping holes of missing strobili; wooden St. Nicholas and sleigh, his painted rosy cheeks chipped and mottled; Meagan's Star of David made from popsicle sticks and garland, the gold filaments crumpled and unraveled. She brought the child's craft to her lips, lovingly kissed the tip, wove the dangling metallic strand back into place. Meagan. Her little girl, who lived among the stars now, shining just as brightly as her creation.

In the corner, knotted, kinked tinsel dripped from ends of the imitation Christmas tree's pine branches. Once, the tang of fresh pine had filled the small house with forest scent, but that was long ago. This symbolic seasonal trimming had been a gift from a friend, a neighbor, who'd taken pity when she'd lost the strength to chop down her own tree. She didn't have the heart to refuse the act of kindness but in her opinion, if it wasn't real, what was the point.

As a show of neighborly civility, the tree went up and later dismantled, year after year until she couldn't be bothered to put it away anymore. Now it held permanent residence, all allure and magic of the holiday trademark gone – just like the people whose souls were woven into the fabric of her life.

A pause between songs gave her a moment to prepare. The first chord was always the hardest. She held her breath. Notes rang out, announcing the song that transported her to a time when life was rich with promises and dreams. Her arms floated into position by their own will, held in the empty embrace of a ghostly lover.

She hummed along with the tune. *O Holy Night*. And it had been. Christmas Eve, nineteen forty-one. Daniel shipped out in two days, so every moment had to be preserved in her memory. They'd danced, sang, loved. Then he was gone. He promised to return and he did, every December twenty-fourth.

In her mind.

She'd patiently wait, set the scene, light the candles, play the music. He never disappointed her. But with each passing year, the sensation of being in his arms grew less and less distinct.

Small, swaying steps took her by the window again. She glanced into the blue-black night and stuttered. With a hand resting against chilly glass she stared, blinked, but her eyes did not deceive. The man's figure was cast in ethereal halo by heaven's lunar orb. He raised a gloved hand, grinned, the mischievous dimpled smile that had always stopped her heart. Dressed in an olive green uniform, he held out his arms in pose, began to dance, twirling in the frosted white carpet beneath his feet. Her raspy phlegm-filled laugh transformed to a soft feminine giggle. Tatty nightgown morphed into a dress of emerald green. When she lifted the hem, looked down, stocking feet became dainty shoes. Bony, veined hands magically encased in black evening gloves opened the door. Biting winter wind turned summer warm, lifted her thin, grey hair and converted it to blond strands like silken wheat. Icy pellets transitioned to warm raindrops, fusing with joyful tears. She ran to him, leapt into his arms. He spun her around, around until they were both dizzy.

She gazed into blue eyes shining with love. "You're back."

He tapped her heart, rested his hand there. "I never left."

And while dots of snow fell like a million white stars, she danced with an unseen partner until the notes of *Oh Holy Night* took her spirit and drifted it towards heaven.

The Battle

The blip, plop, of water dripping off a paddle was the only sound Nancy heard as she guided the canoe out onto the calm lake. Nature's hushed essence enveloped her in the surrounding blackness. A pocket of mist hovered over the lake and she sat with eyes closed, wishing the vapor was the breath of a lover as it tickled fine hairs on her skin like a mystical caress.

The paddle rested across the canoe sides and the craft's almost imperceptible rocking lulled her, its soothing motion pacifying as it would a child; in security and complacent naiveté that the world was just, right, and true.

When she opened her eyes and stared heavenward, she searched for answers to questions haunting her. Not the philosophical age-old quest of 'why am I here?' but 'how can I be here?' How could she gaze at the millions of stars gracing the skies for millennia when the other could not? The other, who was wise, loving, sacred; who was mother, child, sister, aunt; who was with her and within her.

Silence broke with a loon call. No response came to the haunting song. Nancy sighed, knowing the burden she must do but suddenly frightened by the finality of it. Once done, there would be no going back. Once done, could not be undone.

She hesitated and her thoughts ventured back to when the world started to teeter; this day that had begun with brilliant sunshine and now ended with darkest sorrow.

* * *

The aroma of freshly brewed coffee wafted through the tiny house. Nancy's unhurried practiced routine was so rote, she could do it with her eyes closed. She scooped muffin batter into tins and after a quick wipe with a cloth at the few errant drops of mixture, put the pan into the oven and set the timer. Her eyes darted to the wall clock and gauged her time before setting out. Half an hour. The muffins would be done just minutes before she had to leave. Perfect.

A muffled noise interrupted the review of her daily tasks. She froze. Her gaze stole to the clock again and belatedly she realized it was Wednesday. Wednesday was early day. How could she have forgotten? Stupid. Stupid.

A hand grabbed her arm above the elbow, squeezed tight. Pain shot up her arm as she was whirled around. Another hand snaked out, struck her cheek, the contact sound echoing around the kitchen.

"How many times have I told you I don't want muffins on Wednesdays!" screeched the woman, rage emanating from icy blue eyes. Sharp, focused, angry eyes.

Nancy shrank back, trying to pull free from the grasp. "Mom, you have muffins every day," she said, her voice non-threatening and neutral.

"Not on Wednesdays, you stupid girl. How many times do I have to explain it to you?" The woman gripped harder, emphasizing her meaning.

Nancy winced.   "Fine then, we can keep them for afternoon tea or perhaps later," she conceded. "What would you like instead?"

"Toast." The woman practically growled the response, released her prisoner and stalked toward the bathroom. "I always have toast."

Nancy massaged her arm where bruising marks began to form. She lifted the lid to the old-fashioned breadbox, took out two slices of whole wheat bread, placed them into the toaster and depressed the button. At the coffee maker, she poured a cup for her mother, who had just returned and sat down at her usual place.

She carefully placed the coffee cup on the table. Her voice lowered; no hint of what happened moments before. "Your toast will be ready in a minute. Would you like jam or honey on it?"

The woman looked up, a hopeful half-smile on her face. "Oh, Nancy dear, wouldn't it be nice to have muffins some morning? It's been so long since I've had them I can't remember what they taste like."

She sighed. It was getting more and more difficult to find some semblance of normalcy while dealing with her mother's dementia. Every day was a constant battle, some worse than others. Ever watchful of the time, she wondered if she'd have to call in sick at work again. On her mother's worst days Nancy was unable to leave her alone and there was a limit to how much she could impose on her neighbors.

The toaster pinged. Nancy pulled out the slices of bread, slid them on a plate, added a knife, the tub of honey and brought them to her mother.

"Here you go. You can put on as much honey as you like. Is there anything else you want before I leave for work?"

With speed belying her age, the woman snagged Nancy's wrist, pinned it to the table, grabbed the knife with the other hand, and turned the blade so the serrated edge lay directly on the vein.

"You're going to leave me aren't you?" she yelled, "Is this my last meal then? Huh? You're going to walk out that door and hope I rot in my own filth!"

Pain flared up Nancy's arm. The blade cut into her skin, drawing beads of blood from the wound. As she tried to make a grab for the knife, she felt it start to sink deeper. Instinctively, self-preservation kicked in. She fisted her left hand and threw her entire weight into the punch to her mother's temple.

The weapon bounced off the table and clattered to the floor. Nancy clamped down on her wrist, ran to the kitchen sink and turned the tap on. As thin ribbons of red washed down the drain, she assessed the damage. Not as bad as she'd expected but it had been close, very close. She sensed rather than heard the presence of someone behind her and whirled to a defensive stance.

"What happened? Did you cut yourself?" Her mother edged closer. "Oh dear, you should tell my daughter Nancy to have a look at that."

"It's nothing, just a scratch. I need to get a band-aid on it. Why don't you sit and finish your coffee and toast." Nancy walked numbly to the bathroom. She found the band-aids, thankful again the cut had merely broken the skin. She stared at her reflection in the mirror and her thoughts went to the future - endless days of uncertainty, never knowing if her mother would be lucid or even comprehend if Nancy was there. Because of their financial situation, she would have to care for this woman...this woman who had once been so loving. She had no money for the medications needed to help deal with this problem and certainly not the funds required for her mother to be placed in a private home.

Nancy saw what her life would become - if the stranger eating breakfast in the other room didn't end it. She gripped the edge of the chipped vanity and knew what had to be done.

* * *

Nancy's eyes rested on the figure lying at the bottom of the canoe. After spending the day with her mother, she'd persuaded the woman to go for a ride in the country, and stopped at a small lake where an old canoe rested on the beach. The warm sunshine had worked wonders, bringing a stretch of peaceful lucidity to the elder. Until it got dark. Then her parent had to be restrained with duct tape Nancy had taken from home.

Her mother mumbled against the gag in her mouth. Nancy didn't remove the cloth, instead lifted the blindfold from her mother's eyes. The blue orbs that met hers were neither lucid nor insane. They were lifeless, as if the soul had already departed.

Not bearing to keep the contact any longer, Nancy focused on the ebony water, as still as a sheet of glass. Her own reflection mirrored back and she saw the same lifelessness, the same empty soulless stare. Was she becoming her mother already? Was what she was contemplating be the final act that would push her soul over the brink, just as surely as she would push her mother's body over a different edge?

Her gaze flicked between her mother and her reflection upon the watery grave. She made a decision. The paddle felt powerful in her grasp.

She stroked slowly back to the shore.

They both had won the battle.

For today.

The Pact

Warm summer night air drifted in with Jeff as he walked into his house, tossed his keys on the small armoire and strode to the front room. His shoulders sagged more from the weight of his conscious than from the hard day's work he'd put in. Was it that same conscious which made him arrive later and later with each progressing day, he thought to himself as he slumped into the waiting chair. Or perhaps the notion of seeing her face, knowing he could never reveal his secret. But deep down inside, Jeff knew the real reason; procrastination of the inevitable event from which there was no escape.

His wife, Maggie, came into the room, her strikingly beautiful, young face slightly lined with fatigue she carefully tried to hide with makeup. Her smile was tremulous; as if she too knew before the night was through they would be at it again, the emotional and verbal tangling which happened with more frequency lately. And yet, her eyes captivated him, their caramel color shining with a love so deep it was what kept him coming home, kept him from going insane.

He knew they would go through the usual routine - the subtle pointed questions, the veiled accusations, until the final relinquishing of defenses when they both silently agreed to let the matter drop.

For now.

She gave him the beer bottle she had carried into the room, opened her mouth to say something, and then thought better of it. He drank deeply, hoping the brew would wash away the acrid taste in his mouth. But it never did.

"You didn't get a rest in today did you?" he asked, although he knew the answer. He could tell. He could always tell. And the fear rising up in him when she looked like this gnawed away at his belly, until he thought he would die from it. Just like she had almost died a few months back while giving birth to their only son. It was something he would never forget and would never live through if it did happen.

"The day sort of got away from me," she replied with a shrug of her shoulders. She knew the answer wouldn't please him but he loved her and she loved him and he would do anything, anything to keep that love.

"You know you're supposed to rest, the doctor said so Maggie. I don't understand why you won't listen to him, or me."

"Things needed to be done around the house Jeff."

"Then leave them for me and I'll do it when I get home. Or, if need be, we'll get a maid."

"A maid! How are we going to afford a maid?"

"I'll get a part time job if I have to," he retorted in a wave of guilt at the dark circles under her eyes.

"Like you don't work hard enough already?"

"Why don't you call your sister to come over and give you a hand?"

"Because Rebecca has three kids, a job and her own household to look after," she said with a flash of temper. "She can't come over here at the drop of a hat to help me."

"I don't care what it takes. I won't have you getting sick again."

"I won't get sick again Jeff."

"But I almost lost you!" he exploded, surged off the chair and stood so close to her she could probably smell his fear.

A tiny wail from the back of the house shattered the moment of tense silence. Maggie clenched her fists. "Now look what you've done! I finally got Jamie to sleep and now he'll be up for hours. Sometimes Jeff, you don't stop to think!" She whirled away and marched out of the room.

"Well dammit," he mumbled as he stalked out the door. He sat on the front steps of his house, the day's heat that had baked into the wood seeping through his jeans. His eye noticed the wood needed to be stained again. Great. Add that to the list. Yet he cherished this house, the one he and Maggie had fallen in love with and spent a year fixing up. The home was his sanctuary and his family the guardians. He listened to the voices of the night, wondering how their relationship had gotten to this point and how they were ever going to get past it.

He watched a figure dressed in black come up the walk and stop at the base of the stairs. The man rested his foot on the first step and smiled amicably. "Good evening Jeffrey. How are we today?"

"Do you see anyone else sitting here next to me?"

"Such wit. Not having a good day?"

"Don't you have somewhere else to be right now?" Jeff hoped. He wanted this guy gone, now, before Maggie came out.

"On the contrary, I am exactly where I wish to be."

"On my doorstep antagonizing me."

"Is that what you think I do? Antagonize you?" The man smirked.

"What else would you call it?"

"I tend to think of it as having a friendly neighborhood conversation."

"Yeah, well I don't feel too friendly right now," he grumbled. "What do you want?"

"What do I usually want Jeffrey?"

"Why do you keep calling me that? Everyone calls me Jeff."

"Ahh yes, the shortening of a name to depict friendship. You know what I want. I am a businessman making sure you keep your end of the bargain." At Jeff's silence, the man continued. "Having regrets already?"

"Let's just say I'm not enthusiastic about the agreement."

"You didn't seem to have a problem at the time. In fact, if I do remember correctly, you were quite eager. That being the case, am I going to receive payment?"

"Yes, you'll get your God damn payment!" he thundered.

"Tsk, tsk, Jeffrey, no need to swear. We are both gentlemen here."

"Not from where I see it," Jeff said as he rose to follow the man to the street.

* * *

Maggie alternated between pacing the floor and watching television but her mind could not concentrate on the show. After she finally got Jamie settled back to sleep, she went out to try and talk to Jeff again, but he wasn't there. She hated when they argued, just hated it. Emotions, already running high, fueled her anxiety. She had a suspicion Jeff was having an affair. Oh, she had no concrete evidence, but the signs were all too apparent - moodiness, the late nights, and the absences after dinner he explained as getting some fresh air by going for a walk. And then there was the real kicker; they hadn't made love since before Jamie was born. Jeff explained he didn't want to hurt Maggie; he wanted to make sure she was physically healthy. Even her sister Rebecca said the same thing when she relayed her suspicions. God, she hoped that's all it was.

Edgy and tense, she considered taking out her flute and playing for a while. Jeff had given the instrument to her as an engagement gift with the stipulation she take lessons. Playing always gave her peace and the instructor she had said her talent was developing quite well.

Maggie checked her watch and seeing it was getting late, decided she needed to rest. Her flute teacher was coming tomorrow and the lessons were always grueling.

* * *

The pattern of late nights and terse comments continued until everything came to a head a month later. Jeff was even more overdue than usual getting home and Maggie had had enough. She concluded he was having an affair with the woman down the street, obviously within walking distance since he never took the car when he went for his so-called walks. She decided to confront him as soon as he got in. She would give him an ultimatum - either tell her what was going on, or she would take Jamie and move in with her sister for a while. The only other option was to stay and have their lives continue on the same destructive course. She didn't think she had the strength.

The sound of a car door slamming brought her head up. She mentally braced for the verbal exchange she knew would be forthcoming.

"Hi hon," Jeff said, shuffling through the door.

"You're really late Jeff, where were you?"

"Working."

"You're always working late," she retorted, noting her harpy tone but unwilling to apologize.

"I put in a lot of hours to provide for you and Jamie."

"What about providing more than money? How about offering your love and time?"

Jeff sighed. "Maggie, I'm not in the mood. Get off my back."

She launched her fists onto her hips. "Okay Jeff, who is she?"

"What?"

"Who is she?"

"Who is who?" he asked, shaking his head. "What are you talking about?"

"You're seeing someone else. I know it."

"Don't be ridiculous."

"I'm not stupid, Jeff. She has to be in the neighborhood."

"There is no other woman."

"You take off after dinner once a week, yet you don't use the car, so she has to be close. Is it the woman at number fifty-six who moved here last year?"

"Maggie, you're way off base. I bet you're just tired. Did you get a rest in today?"

"No! No! You're always hammering me about getting my rest. Next thing you'll want me to start taking pills to make sure I get enough sleep." Images of her husband with another woman ramped up her temper. "You never arrive home on time anymore. What, a couple of hours not enough time with her?"

A crimson tide flushed Jeff's face. He walked up to her and softly said in a menacing tone, "That's enough."

"Tell me then, where do you go?"

"I don't go anywhere."

"You leave the house, you have to go somewhere. Tell me Jeff. Tell me!"

"It's none of your god-damned business!" he roared and stalked out the door, slamming the portal behind him.

Maggie stood there trembling, heart breaking, her world slipping out from under her. This was how it had to be, she thought. She'd call Rebecca to come get her and Jamie. Her thoughts were already on what to pack for a few days, the rest she would return for later. A tear slid down her cheek when she realized she was already thinking of the inevitable. A second tear followed the first and she walked to the baby's room, choking back the emotional pain threatening to smother her.

* * *

Jeff stood outside seething with rage. Not at Maggie, but at himself. He wanted to tell her, wanted to allay her fears of what was going on. But he knew he couldn't. Not now, not ever.

As if on cue, the man walked down his sidewalk. "Jeffrey, out here again."

"Where else would I be?"

"You look a bit stressed. Everything all right?"

"Just peachy," he ground out. "What are you doing here? Today is not the day."

"I noticed you sitting out here and came over to see if you wanted to talk."

"Nothing to talk about."

"Oh really," the man smirked. "Seems to me you need somebody to talk to since you cannot speak to your wife."

"Leave her out of this."

"Ahhh but isn't she what all *this* is about, our conversations, our meetings?"

"What do you want from me?" Jeff said in defeat.

"Why do you ask a question to which you already know the answer? What I want from you will never change unless you decide it will. You have a choice to make Jeff. We can continue the way things are or you can change it."

Because of his love for Maggie and Jamie, Jeff knew his life would never change and it was a decision he made with confident finality. No matter what happened to him, that would never vary. It was his love for them which had put him in this situation; his endless devotion for his wife had made him turn a corner, made him sacrifice his body and soul so she would live.

His mind went back to the night when Jamie was born. The doctors were losing Maggie on the table while she was giving birth. They had no explanation and were trying everything to save her, but she was slipping away. So, Jeff went to find someone who had the power to save her. And when he did, he paid the price.

With his soul.

A soul for a soul was what the terms of the agreement stated and he gave his for her life. Payment came every week – relinquishing an hour of his soul for a week of her life. Many times Jeff had come close to telling Maggie the truth so she would understand what he did, why he endured the indescribable things done to him, but strings attached to the agreement made him keep eternally silent. If he ever told anyone of the agreement, he would lose Maggie and his son Jamie, forever. They would belong to Him.

Jeff looked at the appearance evil had taken. "Isn't it a bit hypercritical to appear in the form of a man? How can you live with yourself?"

"I take on many forms. And as for live? I do not live. I exist. I exist because mankind does. I am the product of all that is in each and every subject of humanity. Take away the greed, the hatred, the envy and I am no more."

"But I didn't want those things."

"True. But with you Jeffrey, you were selfish. You did not want your precious Maggie to die; could not bear to live if she did not. You chose to change the natural order of things and with any choice there is responsibility for your actions." The man straightened as a car drove up the street. "In the end you have lost anyway. Your sister-in-law is here to take your precious Maggie away. I will see you next week, at the usual time."

"She may not be a part of my life anymore," Jeff uttered with conviction, "but she sure as hell won't be part of yours."

* * *

The house felt like a tomb. Not because of the silence, but because of the loss, resignation and defeat. Maggie worked quickly to pack the remainder of things she hadn't taken when she first left, items that would help her continue on with her life. Life? She was no longer living, merely existing. Without Jeff, the only reason she kept going was because of Jamie.

No matter how long she would ponder over what had happened and why, she knew there was nothing she could ever do to change it.

The knock on the door brought her out of her musings and she went to open it. Her flute teacher, a small, aged woman with a mop of grey curly hair smiled in greeting.

"Good afternoon Maggie."

"Oh. It's you. Have you come to gloat?" Maggie stepped aside to allow the woman to enter then quickly shut the door.

"Well, from the looks of all these boxes I gather you won't be getting back together with Jeffrey after all," the woman cackled.

"How observant. What do you want? Today is not the day."

"I stopped by to make sure you keep your end of the bargain and continue with our 'lessons'. Didn't want to think you might be running out on me. I gather you've told your sister about our arrangement since you will be staying with her until you get back on your feet, dear."

The pact. The deal she made to get the one thing she couldn't live without. Jeff. From the moment she'd laid eyes on him years ago, Maggie knew he was the one. The only problem was he didn't know she existed, just like everyone else. All her life she'd faded into the background; always the last to be picked for teams; never invited to parties; never asked out on a date. The typical ugly duckling. Then along came Jeff and he was all that mattered. He became her obsession. She would do anything to have him, pay anything to have him.

And she did.

"But he no longer loves me, so the contract becomes void," she argued.

"There was never a stipulation on how long Jeffrey would love you. When you took your wedding vows, it was till 'death do you part'. It is amazing what we do for love. You chose to change the natural order of things, Maggie, and for any choice there is responsibility for your actions. For making Jeffrey fall in love with you, I get an hour of your soul every week. Just remember dear, if you tell anyone, I get you, your sister's and Jeffrey's soul."

Visions of interminable years at the hands of evil threatened her resolve. Knowing that Jamie and Rebecca would be safe and yes, even Jeffery, despite how things ended between them, is what gave Maggie strength. "God, I hate you," she spat as she stalked to the door. "Get out."

"God has nothing to do with it, my dear. See you in a few days."

A Precious Glimpse in Time

The late December night's cold air snaps at my cheeks, making them tingle, reinforcing that I am alive. I long for the warm cocoon of my vehicle back at the roadside but once my heartbeat accelerates from trudging through the foot of freshly fallen snow, my body warms and I continue on.

My breath shows as puffs of steam and I idly wonder if I can create smoke rings like my grandfather did from his pipe as he regaled me with stories of long ago whilst I sat upon his knee. It is a foolhardy notion, one best left to children who still think all is possible and wishes make dreams come true.

I am alone on this wintry evening; no other noise assails my ears but the crunch of snow beneath my feet, the huff of my breath in the air. The peaceful stillness is comforting, assuaging ragged emotions which always bombard me at this time of year.

It is Christmas Eve and although I stare up into the night sky littered with diamonds, I do not see the bright star, no guiding light, no messenger to herald the day to come.

After a few moments, I arrive at the edge of my destination. There are paths leading in both directions. I turn left, walking in footprints of those previous to me. The trail meanders to and fro and I follow it until it is time for me to veer off. I lay new tracks, pushing through snow until I reach the other end of the clearing just below a huge oak tree. I stop, catch my breath, stand still to center myself and bring an image to my mind. The picture is one easily captured, brought out and visited at this time of year, at this time of day.

A smile crosses my face as I close my eyes to block out sensory invasions and immerse myself in the memory. The image fills me. I relive the sights and sounds of a precious glimpse in time to a night similar to this, yet vastly different. I feel the memory of her beside me. The puffs of her breath mirror mine as we walk quietly through nature's white blanket, arm in arm, heart to heart. Large, fluffy flakes cascade down as we marvel at the universe's beauty in creating perfect moments. She grabs my hand, clasps it tight. No words are necessary to portray the love she feels for me shining from her eyes, her smile, her soul. I squeeze back in response and we continue on our walk, forever grateful for each other. It is rare, these stolen moments, when it is just the two of us with no other demands of time or attention. Wallowing in the freedom from domesticity, we continue on as snow gently falls.

All too soon the memory fades and her image shimmers away into the night. I open my eyes, sigh heavily, feeling lost and alone. A tear trickles down my icy cheek, warming its path across my skin. Leaning down, I brush snow away from the headstone to make a spot for flowers I brought with me. I carefully unwrap the delicate red carnations from their protective covering, place them on the grave, knowing it was foolhardy to bring fresh flowers in winter. A notion best left to children who still think all is possible and wishes make dreams come true.

"Merry Christmas," I whisper, rising to glance heavenward, looking for peace, looking for her. I linger a moment longer before turning to make my way back to the car. As I leave the tiny cemetery, large fluffy snowflakes cascade down from a cloudless winter sky.

My Life

There is calmness in routine, one I look forward to every morning, the sedate, structured balance of dependability that settles me in preparation of the day. Even before I open my eyes, my senses spring forth, recognizing my surroundings, enfolding me in comfort.

Smell, the strongest sensation, is always first to greet me. The heavenly aroma of fresh coffee pulls a memory of catching the first rays of sunlight cresting over a mountain lake while wisps of steam rising from my cup, lift, dissipate, like the early morning fog off the water.

The sound of thumping feet brings an inner smile – Jason racing down the stairs, ready for his bowl of cereal before rushing off to school. The kid has so much boundless energy. I wait for the usual response from my wife, her love-filled admonishment that he not run in the house and am happy to note she does not disappoint. Later, when Jason gets home, he'll probably zip to my side, spin tales of his adventures with a Jules Verne flair before sprinting outside to play. I can't wait. For now, cupboard doors bang shut, pots rattle, silverware tinkle, the preparations of breakfast for the rest of the family.

The door opens and I get a drift of Lila's citrus shampoo, a fresh innocent scent, like the young woman that she is. She remains in the doorway, as if indecision has anchored her there and I wish she would come, sit beside me and speak her woes, use me as a sounding board. But she doesn't. Instead I hear her soft sigh, filled with anguish before she turns and closes the door quietly behind her.

My heart breaks.

My eyes flutter open and the lack of yellow swaths of illumination on the ceiling indicates it must be cloudy outside. Perhaps we'll get rain. Good, because the garden probably needs it. Mother Nature hasn't given us a real downpour in a while.

I must have dozed off because the next thing I hear is Janice walking in. I follow her path to the bed. The shape of her body still infuses me with sexual hunger despite two children and the dependable familiarity of many years together. She's wearing a snug knit top which mould her breasts and all I can think of is how much I want her, now, regardless of the time of day, the trials of our marriage.

Or maybe because of them.

She leans over me and her favorite perfume swirls its enticing scent up my nose. I try to relay my desire for her through my eyes as she gently lifts my head, fluffs my pillow.

"Morning handsome." She smiles, kisses my lips.

The contact is fleeting and I crave more of its recognizable caress but am left wanting.

My name is Eric, I have ALS and this is my life.

The Justice Box

The carnival's swirling lights and shrieks from the attending crowd assaulted Kailey's senses. She staggered back from a group of girls passing by and shook her head at the stupidity of coming here in the first place. She should be back at home, where she was needed, where she belonged, where she always was. She should never have listened to her neighbor Mavis' insistence to take a break and go out. She should have stayed home and looked after her ailing father, like she had been for the past eight months. Eight long, torturous months of watching him slip farther and farther away no matter what she did to stop it; monitoring the air regulator to make sure he was getting enough oxygen into his lungs; observing his skin turn from a healthy robust pink to ashen grey; watching the life drain from his eyes.

Kailey moved into the shadows of a tent so the carnival revelers could not see her unshed tears. They were always there, those tears, hiding in the background, waiting, always waiting for an unguarded moment to break free. Kailey refused to let her father see her cry. He depended on her to keep the house up and cook his meals, even though he was practically wasting away to nothing. It was just so damn frustrating because there wasn't a way to stop the illness from winning. Well, there was. But they didn't have the money.

Kailey scrubbed away the errant tears creeping down her face and cleared her throat. She was made of stronger stuff. She could care for the house and her father; she had to. Dad had depended on her once mom died. She hadn't let him down then and she would not start now. She zipped up her jacket a bit farther to ward off the crisp fall chill and pulled on her gloves. A waft of popcorn fragranced air enticed, making her mouth water.

"Instead of wallowing in self pity girl, you've been given the opportunity to take a break. Better not waste it," she mumbled in soft admonishment as she entered the flow of people mingling within the fairgrounds.

Kailey continued on her mindless exploration, avoiding carnies trying to get visitors to part with their money. She reached into the pocket of her faded jeans and felt reassurance at the few crumpled bills Mavis had shoved into her hand before pushing her out the door.

"A young woman like you needs to get out and enjoy yourself, every once in a while," Mavis had said when Kailey tried to give back the money. "I don't want to hear any more about it. The carnival is only here for three days and who knows when something that much fun will get to these parts again. Go out and have a good time and I don't want to see you back here before eleven, do you hear?"

She smiled at the image of Mavis standing in the doorway, hands on hips, trying to look intimidating; the stern bluster actually made her more endearing.

Kailey veered towards a dimly lit area of the fairgrounds, lured by the soft tinkle of wind chimes carried on the wisp of a breeze. She found the source of fairy-like notes hanging from a tent decorated with brightly colored scarves. The delicate pieces of fabric fluttered gaily in the breeze, dancing in the air like magic. She stopped at the tent and smirked slightly. A fortuneteller, of course. Every carnival had to have one, it was standard.

The sandwich-board listed rates for palm readings, tarot cards and séances. The usual crap Kailey thought, walking away, but some small lettering at the bottom of the sign caught her eye. 'Your wishes come true – guaranteed or it's free.'

"Now how can you guarantee a person's wishes come true," she muttered. No one could do that. Yet the sign enticed her, called to her, dared her to go inside and find out. "What the hell, as long as it doesn't cost me anything."

She stepped inside. The tent flap drop closed behind her, sending the harsh carnival cacophony into a muted background noise. She was surprised the characteristic Zen-like music, incense, lit candles, and crystal ball were replaced with tables decorated in an assortment of intricate boxes. At the center table sat not the expected gypsy woman wrapped in harem style garb and jingling bangles, but a man, shorter in stature, with olive colored skin, possibly of Egyptian or Indian descent. He had short dark hair and wore small, black round glasses, perched at the end of his nose as he gazed at the luminescent stone in his hands.

"Good evening." He spoke softly, his slightly accented voice rich and warm. He smiled at her and held up the stone he was examining.

"Beautiful, isn't it?"

"Yes, it's gorgeous. What kind of stone is it?"

"A worship stone. Very rare. I have just recently received it and had, as yet, not been able to examine it."

Kailey stepped closer so the man could place the stone in the palm of her hand. She fingered its smoothness and wondered at the tiny speckles of light it radiated. "What is it for?"

"It is given as a gift to people we worship," he explained, retrieving the item and slipping it into the pocket of his jacket. "Now, is there something I can do for you?"

Flustered at being caught enamored by something as silly as a rock, Kailey jerked her thumb toward the tent opening. "The sign says you guarantee my wish to come true," she said with skepticism.

"Yes, that is true."

"Yeah, okay. So, what's the gimmick?"

The man gestured for her to sit across from him. "Obviously there is something you wish that made you put curiosity aside and venture into my tent," he said when she started to refuse, "There is no trick, really."

He walked to the corner, retrieved a small intricately carved chest and returned to the table, placing the chest directly in front of her.

"What's this?" she asked with rising curiosity as he sat back down.

"It is a justice box."

"A justice box?"

"Correct."

"What exactly is a justice box?"

"I think it would be easier if it was demonstrated, rather than explained. Think of some small item you would like to have but is not in your possession."

"Look, how much is this going to cost?" Kailey interrupted him, sensing the probability of a scam. This place was part of a carnival, a whole industry based on illusion.

"There is no cost. This is only the demonstration. If you feel you do not wish to have the justice box, you are free to leave. The box works like this - you will ask it to give you what you wish and it will ask for something in return."

"What, now the box can speak?" she laughed.

"You have nothing to lose. Please. Sit back and in your mind think of some small item you would like to have but do not possess."

"Can it be anything at all?" Despite her desire to keep things in perspective, her pulsed jumped. She had nothing to lose, just like the man said.

"Yes, it can be anything which might fit in the box. But bear in mind, the justice box will ask for something in return it deems is of equal value."

Kailey gazed at the black box. It was almost perfectly square, slightly larger than a shoebox and was detailed with foreign carvings. She had never seen anything quite like it before and to her, the markings didn't look like something from the Asian or Egyptian culture.

"How do I know you don't have this rigged or something?"

He smiled good naturedly. "If it makes you feel better, bring the box closer to you and look inside."

She did and saw the unit, lined in red velvet, was totally empty.

"Now, keeping it in your hands, think of the item. Once you have the image in your mind, say the words 'Give me what I wish for.'"

"You're sure this isn't going to cost me anything?"

"Not a thing. This is only a demonstration. But if you wish to keep the item, the box it will ask for something in return."

She gazed at the box, entranced by its designs. Her fingers gently traced indentations, curves and swirls, as if caressing the carving could bring them to life. She closed her eyes and focused on the object in her mind she purposely picked because it could not possibly be put in the box. Her desire was frivolous, something she would never get for herself. However, if she could, she would love to have the pair of gorgeous silver shoes she saw in the new store in town. She could never afford them and truth be known, there were not a lot of places she could wear them. Yet when she saw the footwear they almost begged to be taken home. Of course, she didn't tell a soul. People would think she was senseless, petty and silly, asking for a pair of shoes when there were bills to pay. But it was fun to be indulgent. She shrugged and spoke the request "Give me what I wish for."

No puff of magic smoke, no thunderous boom. Not even a good kick-up of wind.

Kailey looked at the man and frowned. "Well, where are they?"

"Open the box," he replied.

She lifted the lid, gasped in surprise. Her eyes narrowed on satin dress pumps. There were her shoes. But, that was impossible, just impossible. How in the hell could they have gotten from the store in town to here in the blink of an eye? And she never let go of the box, so there was no way the man could have slipped them in there. Besides, how could he have known?

"I gather from the look on your face, you have received what you wished for?'

All she could do was nod her head.

"Now the question to you is, do you wish to keep them?"

"But I don't have the money."

"The justice box will not ask for money," he explained. "When you close the lid and ask it 'what do you wish for,' it will reveal the payment."

"What happens then?" she inquired, more caught up in the magic than ever, her initial reluctance and disbelief gone.

"If you should decide to keep the item, the box will ask for payment. When payment is received, the box is yours. You may keep it for as long as you like. At any time you may ask for one wish, but only one wish. Once you have received whatever you wish for, you have one week to deliver payment."

"Whom do I give the payment to?"

"As the current owner, the restitution comes to me, whatever it is, both now and for your one wish in the future."

Kailey thought of the possibilities for the box's use. Her mind wandered to her father, so deathly ill. Maybe there was a way to help him. Maybe the box would be able to provide the answer.

"Has the box ever failed?"

"It will always deliver what you ask. But you must be specific. You need to picture in your mind what you want."

She took a deep breath and was just about to accept the offer when the man placed his hand on her arm. "There are a few rules."

She knew it. Here it comes, the hook making this totally unobtainable. "Go on."

"Again, I must stress you have one week to produce payment for whatever you wish for."

"What happens if I don't?"

"You will die."

She gaped at him. That was nuts. She wasn't going to put her life on the line for a wish from some stupid box. But... what if it did work? What if it gave her the medicine her father so desperately needed? Would that not be worth taking the risk? Her father had always there for her, sacrificing many things so she could have a better life. Could she not do the same? Besides, she would only die if she didn't produce the payment. Maybe she wouldn't have ask the box for anything. She could take it now and ff he father got better she wouldn't have to worry.

"What if I never wish for anything?"

"Then the box stays in your possession until you give it to another. But to give it to another, they must wish for something and produce payment to you, like we are doing now."

"Can't I just leave it somewhere, destroy it or throw it out?"

The soft spoken man shook his head. "You will die. The box must always be transacted to another."

The air surrounding her felt stuffy, enclosed, almost smothering. Kailey had always taken the safe route, followed the path expected of her. Would she ever be able to take a chance and wish for the medicine to help cure her father? If she found she could not do it, couldn't take that plunge, she could always give the box to the next person and then deal with her conscience.

"Once you have agreed to keep the shoes and remitted payment, the box is yours to do with what you wish. If you decide not to do anything, that is fine. However, it must pass from your possession to another before you die. If it does not, someone else close to you will perish. Remember, to give it to another, they must ask for a possession and the box will ask for payment within a week, which will be given to you. The new owner must be made aware of the risks before they take possession. The justice box will *always* give you what you request and never ask for money as payment." The man stopped and gazed deeply into her eyes. "Make a decision. Do you wish to keep the shoes, produce the fee it requires and take possession of the box? Or, will you walk away with a fanciful story to tell your friends?"

Kailey nibbled on her lower lip, her heart thumping against her ribs. It sounded too good to be true. But she saw with her own eyes that the box worked. If it could get the medicine her father needed, she had no choice but to take possession of it.

Taking a deep breath, she drew the box to her again and spoke "What do you wish for?" She waited, an eternity stretching with each second, and lifted the lid. Inside was a small slip of paper. 'Your gloves for payment' stared back at her in block letters. Practically wilting with relief, she reached into her jacket pocket, took out her gloves and laid them on the table.

"Since I promised the transaction was only a demonstration, it is my right as the owner to give you back your gloves. The justice box is now yours. Use it wisely." He smiled but Kailey couldn't see any hint of malice. Maybe this would work after all.

She thanked the man for the return of her gloves, placed the silver shoes in the box. At the opening of the tent, she cast a last look at the intriguing man. He nodded once at her unspoken question and she hurried out. It was late, and she'd stayed much longer than expected. Keeping a tight hold on her new prize, she walked briskly towards the nearest exit, a spring in her step for the first time in a very long while.

* * *

Over the next few days, Kailey kept busy winterizing the house and caring for her father. Between running errands, changing bedding and cooking meals, time slipped away. Before she knew it, the carnival departed, leaving stray flyers tacked to a few poles, paper edges snapping in the stiff fall wind. The justice box, however, was never far from her mind. It sat on the dresser in her room, waiting for a wish. Occasionally she would pick the thing up, think about items that would help them out, but her thoughts invariably turned toward the medicine. Oddly enough, her father showed no further signs of deterioration. Hope blossomed.

When nature's white blanket lowered, things changed. Kailey's father began to slip away, his health failing, his life ebbing. She stood by anxiously, waiting for a miracle; waiting for something to assuage the weight of responsibility, anything to take away the decision that was always in the back of her mind. All she wanted was a sign to give her the courage to stretch beyond her boundaries and take that final step.

Eventually, she couldn't wait any longer. Time had come for her to make her choice. If she did not wish for the medicine that would help her father, he'd die and Kailey would have done nothing to stop it. Racked with indecision, her thoughts never strayed from the justice box for more than a few moments. Even Mavis had commented on her lifelessness, and that Kailey had almost stopped eating. She couldn't go on like this. Her fear was devouring her alive. She had to make a decision.

Her hands shook as she took the justice box from the dresser onto her lap and sat on the bed. She had been dreading this day. Not because she didn't believe the justice box would be able to produce the medicine. Of that she had no doubt. No, what plagued her, what haunted her dreams at night, garnered her almost every waking thought was what form of payment the justice box would demand. The man said it would ask for what it deemed to be of equal value. Did that mean it would ask for another life? Would it be hers? Or Mavis'?

"But which decision," she wailed to the empty room. Would she be able to choose a life over her father's? Would she have to kill another for his life? Isn't that what the bible had said, an eye for an eye? Would she do it? Could she do it? Did she have a choice?

"Help me," she sobbed, clutching the justice box close to her heart, begging for an answer.

Her father's muffled cry of pain broke into her misery and she ran from the room, leaving the justice box on the bed. She strode quickly to his bedside, took his frail hand, caressing it gently.

"I'm here dad."

"My dear Kailey," her father's reedy voice rasped. "I could always rely on you. You've given up so much to take care of me. Maybe it's time, honey."

"No, dad," she replied emphatically.

"It's okay sweetheart. I'm not scared. You need to live. You need to enjoy life. Get married, have children. My life is done. It's time for you to live yours."

"Dad, no! What are you saying? You're not going to give up on me." She almost yelled, panic stuttering her heartbeat. He was scaring her. Since he became ill he had refused to succumb to the possibility the disease would win. And now, now when all she needed was just a little bit of courage he was letting go.

"Wait dad, you have to wait. Just wait and I'll be right back," She was sobbing now, grasping her father's hand.

"It's okay Kailey, let me go." He held on, gave her fingers one last squeeze. "I love you honey."

And then the frail hand went slack, slipping onto the bed. For a fraction of a second Kailey stared in denial before a wail of anger, at the disease, at herself, ripped from her soul. "Noooo. No dad, not yet! Come back! I can get the medicine. Dad! Dad!"

Deathly silence remained. She dropped onto the floor, curled into a ball and wailed like the lost child she was, rocking back and forth as a river of unshed tears swept away time.

* * *

Four months passed since her father died. Kailey had stayed in the house, barely venturing out except for provisions. Her life ceased to exist and she blamed herself for her father's death. It was her reluctance to take a leap of faith and the unknown that would have, and probably could have, saved her father's life. And every night she glared at the evidence of her cowardice on the dresser. She had often contemplated destroying the justice box. She had no use for it now. But in the back of her mind, she believed her father would be disappointed in her. Because, in essence, the box's destruction would mean her suicide. It would mean she wasn't strong enough to carry on. And even though her father was no longer with her in body, she believed he was there in heart and spirit and she just couldn't do it. She just couldn't end her life for that reason.

On an early spring day, with the sun trying to push away the last of winter's hold, Kailey had a yard sale and one of the items on display was the justice box. Since she knew she would never use it now, the gift of its power would be wasted on her. Therefore, it was time to pass it onto another owner. She kept a close eye on the item. Quite a number of people commented on the ornate square but they did not show an intense curiosity for it, like she had. As the morning meandered into early afternoon, and prospective bargain hunters started to thin, Kailey set to the task of assembling a donation box of the belongings that hadn't sold. She was in the middle of that task when a car pulled into the driveway. The lone occupant stepped out of the late-modeled vehicle and ventured forward.

"Hi. Guess I'm a little late," the young woman said in a quiet tone. A simple gingham dress hung loose on her slight frame. Her only adornment was a thin wedding band and an ivory cameo around her neck.

"Just starting to pack up. There are still lots of things you can look through. Is there anything in particular you wanted?" Kailey asked.

"Do you have anything for a child? I'm looking for some toys he can play with in bed. Or maybe some stuff for drawing?" She absently fingered the cameo.

Kailey nodded to the piece of jewelry. "That's very pretty. It looks quite old."

"It was my great grandmothers'."

"Must mean a great deal to you."

"Yes, family is everything," she said.

Kailey noted the strained look on the stranger's face, the haunted expression in her eyes.

"Umm, I don't really have anything suitable for children. I don't have any myself. But I might have an old paint set here somewhere." Kailey rushed on when she saw disappointment lay like a heavy blanket on the woman's drooped shoulders. "And I think I actually might have a paint-by-number set from years ago. I'm not sure if a child could do it. What age is your son?"

The stranger's features softened immediately, her eyes filling with love. "Rickie is eight. Coming up on nine in the fall." She faltered, turned away and wrapped her arms around her thin body.

"Are you all right? Is something wrong?"

"Sorry. It's just really hard. Rickie has a disease the doctors can't seem to figure out. They don't have any answers. He's at home now. He can't go to school. But oh my, that boy loves to draw." A wistful smile edged the corners of her mouth.

As if meant to be, Kailey knew this was the person who would be the next owner of the box. She had to convince this woman that if there was a chance, any chance to save her son she needed to take it. *Had* to take it. For all their sakes.

"Actually, I may have just the thing for you. Come over here, I want to show you something." Kailey placed the justice box in the ladies' hand.

"Oh wow, it's beautiful. What is it?"

"It's called a justice box and I think it might be the answer you're looking for."

"Why are you showing me this? Does it have paints inside?" She lifted the lid.

"If you had a guarantee your son would be cured, what would you give?"

"That's not funny," the woman snapped, shoving the box back into Kailey's hands.

"I'm not joking. If I told you this box has the power to give you anything you wish for, no matter what it is, what would it be worth to you?"

"I don't have that kind of money," she practically cried.

"I'm not talking about money. This is a justice box. You wish for one thing, anything, and it is granted. All you have to do is provide payment."

"I told you I don't have any money." The stranger headed back to her vehicle.

"Wait!" Nothing mattered to Kailey now except to help this woman. "The box does not ask for money" she stressed and spent the next half hour explaining how the box worked, what the rules and risks were. She even explained how she became the owner of the box, what she had wished for and what the payment was. But she couldn't bring herself to tell the visitor what she didn't have the courage to wish for. She hoped this woman had the strength she lacked.

After a long silence in which the stranger examined the box and gave careful consideration to the responsibilities, she nodded.

"I'll take the box," she stated with a tremor in her voice.

"Did you want to ask for something small, sort of like a demonstration? You know that once you accept the gift the box is yours and you can use it again, but only once."

"I know. But I don't want to take any chances. I am willing to pay whatever the price is to save my son. If it is my own life, I am willing to die for him."

For a moment Kailey hated and envied the person standing there, for her faith, her conviction. Yet, she also admired this woman's strength because Kailey could only imagine what the box would consider equal to the life of a child.

The woman took the justice box and closed her eyes. She was silent for so long Kailey wondered if she'd had second thoughts, but a quiet plea could be heard on whispered words. "Give me what I wish for."

For one heart wrenching minute the world felt like it had stopped turning. Kailey held her breath as the lid was opened. A sob of delight told her everything she needed to know. The miracle was true. The visitor reached in, retrieved a small vial of clear liquid plus a syringe as tears cascaded down her face.

"I have to ask you now," Kailey cautioned past the lump threatening to close off her throat, "do you accept this gift? If so, you are required to produce payment and the justice box then becomes yours. Do you understand?"

"Yes." No hesitation, no fear. Just awe.

"Are you sure about this?" Kailey placed her shaking hand on the lid of the box. She was scared for this woman - scared she would comply and terrified she wouldn't.

"With all my heart," she said and held the box close. "What do you wish for?"

They waited and peered inside. A slip of paper sat at the bottom, black letters stark against pure white. The words blurred, Kailey looked away, her eyes awash in tears. She felt like she was dying, crumbling into nothingness and that her soul would dissolve away into the spring breeze. The scream building in her body was blocked behind her hand covering her mouth.

The stranger reached to the back of her neck, unhooked the cameo and placed it into Kailey's hand along with the note. She folded Kailey's hands into her own and kissed them.

"Thank you," she said with love and walked to her car.

As the woman drove away, upbeat tune from the radio blasting out the windows, the justice box on the passenger seat beside her, she did not hear Kailey's scream of madness as she crumpled to the dirt.

About the author

Pat is a playwright and award winning author who has had a love affair with the written word since childhood, many times immersing herself in the stories of Enid Blyton and Carolyn Keene. An active imagination gave inspiration to short stories and her first play as a teen.

Her full-length play *The Truth About Lies* was staged at a regional theatrical competition in 2006. She was selected in the "One of 50 Authors You Should Be Reading" contest in 2012. One of her novels achieved a finalist slot in the 2013 International Book Award Contest - fantasy category. She was also one of the winners of the 15th Annual Writer's Digest Short Story Competition for *A Holy Night*.

Although still in pursuit of a place truly called home, Pat shares her life with her husband and three cats, all of which claim rule over the house at one point or another. Besides dreaming up her next novel, Pat enjoys traveling, baking, camping, wine and or course reading - not necessarily in that order.

You can find her on Facebook, her website

patriciaclee.com or send her an email at authorpatriciaclee@yahoo.com